ALSO BY MAURICE BROADDUS

THE KNIGHTS OF BRETON COURT SERIES

King Maker

King's Justice

King's War

The Knights of Breton Court (omnibus)

Orgy of Souls (with Wrath James White)

I Can Transform You

The Voices of Martyrs (collection)

BUFFALO SOLDIER

MAURICE BROADDUS

A TOM DOHERTY ASSOCIATES BOOK

NEW YORK

This is a work of fiction. All of the characters, organizations, and events portrayed in this novella are either products of the author's imagination or are used fictitiously.

BUFFALO SOLDIER

Cover illustration by Jon Foster
Cover design by Christine Foltzer

Edited by Lee Harris

A Tor.com Book
Published by Tom Doherty Associates
175 Fifth Avenue
New York, NY 10010

www.tor.com

Tor® is a registered trademark of
Macmillan Publishing Group, LLC.

ISBN 978-0-7653-9428-6 (ebook)
ISBN 978-0-7653-9429-3 (trade paperback)

First Edition: April 2017

P1

For my Mom
Thanks for all of the stories
(I was listening even when you thought I wasn't)

I.

Move Out of Babylon

DESMOND COKE PINCHED a clump of chiba leaves from his pouch and rolled it into the fine pressed paper. He was down to his last few leaves, perhaps enough for one or two more sacraments before he'd be down to stems and seeds. He sat alone underneath a cotton tree, lit his spliff, and dreamt of home. Exhaling a thin cloud of smoke, he leaned against its gray trunk. The dried brown vines draping it crunched beneath his movement. Under the strange western sky, the dark and loathsome trees crowded the hillside. Before bedtime, his mother used to tell him stories of how *duppies* danced among their branches or hid among the caves. If he'd been particularly troublesome that day, she'd tell him of the powerful spirit, Old Higue, and how the creature would hang her skin along the branch of a cotton tree before she went about her grim business. The tree reminded him of home, but he was far from the shores of Jamaica. They both were.

From a distance, the mountains reminded him of Garlands. Homes tucked in clusters, their boarded windows empty and dark. Beneath the midnight foothills, a town spread out like an uneven smear. Without the constant tropical sun, without the music, without the sea air, without the smell of jerk chicken or rice and peas or ackee and saltfish, without the people, it was just another craggy hill. A fading ghost memory of another life.

A river bordered the vast forest. Desmond inched down the hillside. His footing slipped in a slide of mud, stopping just above the riverbank. They followed the river through the Tejas Free Republic, dressed as a migrant worker and his son. The plan was to elude any Albion intelligence by becoming lost within the seaport in Louisiana, ease across the border, and follow the river north into the Five Civilized Tribes territory. Perhaps travel up into Canada. Wherever they could start over, unknown, without a past and without pursuers. He had not counted on tensions between Albion and Tejas flaring up again. The local newspaper declared that Regent Clinton threatened to mobilize federal agents in the Tejas standoff. They barely eluded the Tejas militia that sealed the borders. A week into their trek, as they kept from major roads, doubt crept in.

Desmond tromped as loud as he dared while nearing their camp. He'd found that the boy was easily startled and sudden noises were prone to sending him into keening fits. The more he could let the boy know that he approached, the smoother things would go. "I'm glad we decided to camp near the water. It's nice here. Plenty of trees for pickney to play in."

Lij Tafari looked up at him with his large, alien green eyes—those not-quite-right green eyes, Desmond once called them—as if struggling to understand the concept of the words. He stroked the fine dirt. "Sand."

"Yes, it looks like sand." Desmond worried about him. He touched Lij on the shoulder to draw his attention. "You need to look me in the eye when you're talking to me."

"I hear you." Lij focused on the dirt, running his hands through it.

"I know you hear me, but . . ." Desmond scrambled for the right words and tone. He never imagined conversation with a child could be so difficult. "I need to know you're listening to me. You're helping me by letting me know you're paying attention to me. Do you understand?"

"No." But Lij lifted his head to meet the man's eyes.

Desmond nodded. "Thank you."

"I want to go for a walk now," Lij said.

"A walk would do you well."

Desmond waved him off. Lij took off his shoes and

ran his toes through the grass. Soon the boy dug in the mud and explored the woods, finding hidden designs and searching for the mysteries of childhood long lost on Desmond. Lij was a gift. Because of the life he had chosen, Desmond never bothered to dream about the possibility of children of his own. Very few things scared Desmond, but only a couple weeks into being a guardian, the very notion of fatherhood terrified him. He had no idea if he was doing it right. All he wanted was to keep Lij safe. That was why they fled Jamaica in the first place. But children needed fresh air, room to play and be children. It was Desmond's burden to worry about food, water, and what kind of life he could provide for his charge.

Desmond emptied their knapsacks and proceeded to hand-wash their clothes. Though Jamaica was a technological rival to Albion in the west, in its hills, in the heart of true Jamaica as Desmond thought of it, some of its people still struggled. He recalled the memories his mother used to share. Of walking six miles to collect water. Of bathing in rivers or showering in rainstorms. Of doing laundry and hanging clothes on the line for the sun to dry. Although, to be fair, his mother wasn't above exaggeration to make her point.

It seemed like a lifetime before when Desmond posed as a servant to draw close to a prominent Jamaican family. Becoming their attaché to better glean their secrets. Living out someone else's mission and calling it his life. He admonished himself when he dwelt too long on his old life. It sent him spiraling into a melancholy mood, one which he couldn't afford if he were going to protect Lij.

"Come nuh," Desmond called out. "It's time to get ready for bed."

Lij trudged back. He checked his shoes as if they might have wandered from where he left them. He lined them up again. Desmond took a washcloth and wiped the boy's face.

"We should figure out how old you are for when people ask. What's a good age?"

"Five." Lij closed his eyes and stiffened when the washcloth went over his face.

"You don't look five."

"How old are you?"

Desmond never knew his own birthdate, nor how many he had celebrated. They had that in common. "Well, let's just say that I'm old. How's seven?"

"Seven. I like seven."

"Seven's a good age. I played in the trees a lot when I was a pickney."

"It's different. There's so much . . . outside." Lij studied the trees as if suspecting that they snuck up on him if he didn't keep a watchful eye on them.

"They didn't let you play?" Desmond had long waited

for the opportunity to broach the topic of the boy's captivity.

"They had a lot of rules. I couldn't go outside. I mostly stayed in a special room."

"What did they have you do?"

"Listen. A man who sounded like me except more . . ."

". . . grown?" Desmond imagined endless speeches. Indoctrination, subliminally learning the speeches and cadence of the man they wanted Lij to become.

"Yes. Old like you."

"Now I'm old, am I?" Desmond smiled.

Lij touched Desmond's mouth and traced the curve of his lips and then mirrored his smile.

"Did they do anything else in the room?"

"Needles." Lij held his breath and closed his eyes like a boy expecting an injection. He opened his eyes and moved on. "Listening to the man was like listening to music."

"Do you like music?"

"Yes. I miss that."

"Me too."

The wind screamed, buffeting the lean-to Desmond had constructed. Having once been a soldier, he'd slept in worse places. But this was no life for a child. He patted his lap. Lij neared him, like a deer checking for the scent of a predator, before laying his head down. Desmond wrapped a thin blanket over him and shut his eyes. Tomorrow would be different. They would foray into town. Perhaps he would look for work. Maybe carve a space for them where they would be unknown, unburdened by their pasts and their history.

The storm-wracked sky held back its rains. Lightning fingers scraped the clouds, threatening in the distance, eventually followed by a low rumble. But that wasn't what kept Desmond awake. It was the dreams. He could never remember them upon waking, only snippets of images and the vague sense of unease. He heard a voice, barely a whisper, though soft and melodic. A woman approached, though he couldn't make out her face. His limbs froze in place. A weight pressed against his chest. Then she was gone, like an errant breeze. He imagined what it felt like to be in *myal,* to have a spirit take hold of him and ride him, like when his people called to their ancestors. When he woke, Lij stared at him, his eyes wide and knowing. The boy rocked back and forth, comforted by his own ministrations. Desmond closed his eyes.

Desmond dreamt of fire.

Under the overcast sky, a pall settled over the town. Heavy plumes of smoke issued from a machine parts manufacturer just outside of town. Any town considered a potential boomtown had encampments whose tents fluttered in the breeze like a squad of sailboats coming to port. People flocked to a town such as this for an opportunity for a factory job. A cloister of lean-tos, bivouacs, and canvas sheets stretched out for shelter formed a tent city that nestled against the town proper. In their travels, Desmond and Lij had run across the occasional barn at night filled with people sprawled along the bales of hay. Entire families huddled together to stay warm. The occasional loner on the hop, following the train lines. A sign swung over the main road.

WELCOME TO ABANDON.

A giant steamman stood under the banner. The occasional oversized steamman dotted the border of Tejas, like huge statues, monuments as warning to trespassers. The units were part of every militia outpost. Over fifteen meters high and seven meters across, the bright silver of the massive structure reflected the sun with such intensity, an overhang had been constructed so that its glare didn't blind drivers. Steam puffed from its back and poured from the chimney that formed its hat. Four men attended it. Their construction fairly crude, such steammen required four people to work the gears and valves to control their lumbering movements. Sweat soaked through the blue uniforms of the attendants, but they remained at parade rest under the afternoon sun like grimy versions of the guards at Buckingham Palace.

His cane tapping along the bricked streets, Desmond strode across the mud-sluiced street, holding Lij's hand. Knapsacks tossed over their shoulders, they accumulated stares as if the townsfolk had never seen black people before. Lij gripped his hand tighter.

A man jostled Desmond as they passed on the walkway. Desmond nodded and kept moving. The man, not satisfied, stopped and doubled back after them.

"You got something to say?" the man asked after him. His face was pocked and rugose. Bulbous, bloodshot eyes, like ebony marbles swimming in a skim of yellow, tracked him. Alcohol wafted on his breath.

Desmond kept walking. The man quickened his steps to get ahead and cut Desmond off.

"I'm talking to you." The sentence stopped short as if leaving a blank for Desmond to fill in with the unspoken word "boy."

Perhaps Desmond wasn't deferential enough in how he carried himself. The townsfolk expected him to avert his eyes rather than meet their gazes full on. He recognized the looks and the ruffled sensibilities. He had only pretended to be a servant back home but had learned the rules of social engagement with one's "betters." Though back home, servants were often treated as extended family, here the spirit of servitude seemed taught as well as ingrained. Borne in the very air to where its spirit was expected in every interaction. Desmond breathed a different air.

"You bumped into me. I excused you. What more was there to say?" Desmond measured his words with care, removing as much of his accent as possible.

"*You* excused *me*? You the uppity sort, ain'tcha?" Anger and resentment undergirded his words, like he'd been waiting for an excuse, an opportunity, to vent both.

"You say that like it's a bad thing."

"You got a smart tongue on you, boy. I may just have to cut it out of you."

The man let his jacket coat fall to the side to reveal the Colt hanging in its holster. Desmond was not dressed, he hadn't carried a weapon since he left Jamaica. Not counting his cane. On some men, a gun was a tool. On others, it was a crutch they depended on too much which gave them a fool's courage. Desmond counted six ways to disarm the man from this position, one of which involved shattering the man's hip in such a way as to give him a permanent limp.

"Gentlemen, gentlemen." Another man sidled toward them. With a green vest and a matching tie, his long jacket a swirl of light green patterns, he seemed a bit of a fop. Yet he carried himself like the top ranker of a gang. "It's too beautiful a day to sully with gratuitous violence.

Can't we just agree that we all have a big one and get along?" The fop turned to the rude man. "Obviously, this man is a visitor to our fine city. Is this any way to introduce him to our hospitality?"

"No, Mr. Hearst." The man spoke in a low, apologetic grumble.

"Why don't you head over to the Redeemer and let them know you're drinking on my tab?"

"Yes, Mr. Hearst." The rude man backed away from them, bumping into the wood column supporting the awning over the walkway, before turning in the opposite direction.

"I apologize for that, gentlemen." The man knelt down to meet Lij's gaze and outstretched his hand. "My name is Garrison Hearst. And who might you be?"

Lij scooted behind Desmond, keeping his guardian squarely between him and the stranger. Desmond felt him tense behind him and slightly tug at his pants leg. Lij had a way of studying people. Like he paid attention to them not quite when he found them interesting, but rather when they were being . . . them. Honest. Real. And his scrutiny had a weight behind it, as if every part of him, every sense, poured over them. Vivisecting them. Mr. Hearst took a step back and withdrew his hand.

"He is my charge," Desmond said. "I am Desmond Coke."

"Pleased to meet you both. I'm as close to the Chancellor of this place as there is. Are you planning on settling in around here?"

"We're passing through."

"The road is a hard life for a boy. You're welcome to stay a spell." Mr. Hearst possessed the well-practiced charm of a politician.

"We're just looking for a room for a night or two. See how things go."

"I recommend the Fountain Hotel. And I insist that you join me for dinner at the Redeemer."

"Having met some of its clientele, this . . . Redeemer doesn't sound like the proper place for a child."

"You are a guest of mine. You have my personal guarantee." Mr. Hearst tipped his top hat so low on his face, it shaded his muttonchops. They watched him amble towards the building across the street.

A row of storefronts lined either side of the main thoroughfare. A series of vendors rose in chorus as they passed, hawking everything from fresh fruit to cleaned chickens. At the end of the street was the city square, with the courthouse, Chancellor's office, and Sheriff's office. On one side of the square stood another imposing steamman. On the other, a gallows. A body dangled from a noose.

"Lord have mercy," Desmond said.

"Strange fruit, indeed." A woman pushed blond strands from her face. A young waif of a girl, no matter how much makeup she wore, whose face hadn't lost all of her baby fat. Her eyes, though, were green and hard. They had a cynical maturity to them, the haunted look of someone who had been alone for a long time. With a blue dress trimmed in fur, despite the heat, she kept the cuffs of her sleeves pressed together, forming a hand muff.

"Excuse me?"

"The body. They found a Pinkerton agent trying to pass as a citizen. That was their judgment."

"Pinkertons work in pairs. They probably left him as warning to the other would-be infiltrators."

"Yeah, remind folks of the limits of the Pinkertons' reach here," she sighed.

"What a world we live in," Desmond muttered, ready to whisk Lij off the street.

Scooting around him, Lij reached up to touch the fur lining of her dress. She kept her eyes on him while she reached into her purse to retrieve a small music box. She opened it. Clockwork gears spun a tiny ballerina. The tinny strains of "Beautiful Dreamer" began.

"Are you new to town?" she asked.

"I must be wearing a sign." Desmond tipped his broad-brimmed, cream-colored straw hat.

"You look like you come from money."

"What makes you say that?" Desmond turned about to study his outfit. A long-sleeve shirt and dungarees with large patch pockets. With his bead necklace, his clothes were like any other laborer from home.

"The way you carry yourself, mostly." She smiled a toothsome grin as if attempting to not embarrass him. "In my profession, you get good at sizing people up quickly."

"And what profession is that?" A high-priced escort was certainly the image she went for, but the way in which she carried herself played more like a story within a story.

"Manners." She swatted him with her fan. "Besides, the accent doesn't help."

"I thought I was doing a passable Albion accent." Desmond stepped back as if smelling his own breath, now self-conscious of his slightly accented English. As an attaché, he often dealt with businessmen from all over the Albion Empire, especially delegates from the Albion colony of America. At the thought, he longed to hear the familiar sing-song patois of his people. From the moment he stepped from the airship depositing them on the United States soil, he'd worked at losing his accent. He had soon tired of the entreaties from perfect strangers for him to "speak Jamaican" for them, as if he were the quirky object for their study. Or amusement. Still, with his accent growing softer and softer with each week, he felt as if he were slowly erasing himself.

"It's passing only if you'd never actually met an Albion citizen."

"But I have. Quite many, actually."

"You're thinking the United States proper, not that what you're doing would fly much out there. But you're in Tejas now. You might as well be speaking a foreign language."

Desmond altered his pitch and cadence. "I'll have to work on it."

The woman scrunched her face as if hearing someone tune a poorly kept instrument. "You can find me at the Redeemer. I'm there often. Any time you want a listening ear, come see me."

As the woman sauntered away from them, Lij relaxed.

"Let's find a room." Desmond gently yanked at his hand. "Get off the streets and away from so many people. These Tejans, they love chat too much."

II.

Black Shadow

LIKE THE REST of the town, the lobby of the Fountain was under renovation. Large white sheets draped the furniture and walls, as if the hotel hosted a gathering of ghosts lounging in odd positions.

"We'd like a room," Desmond said.

"Passing through or staying for a while?" The concierge had a thick mustache and a patch of hair on his chin. He smoothed down errant tufts of hair with his palm. Despite a vest and jacket, his shirt was unbuttoned and filthy about the collar. A long watch chain dangled from his jacket pocket to his vest.

"Tonight for now. We'll see what tomorrow brings."

"Right." Glancing between Desmond and the boy, the man's eyes betrayed him mentally putting his thumb on the scales. "That'll be one hundred credits. In advance."

"I see." Desmond fished in his change purse. Their funds were running low. He would need to find work soon or risk them begging in the streets. He withdrew a Jamaican bank note. A five-hundred-dollar bill with a portrait of Grandy Nanny on it. One of the freedom fighters who drove away Albion forces from the Jamaican shores during the Maroon Wars. Like an important part of his history, he held on to it. A reminder of a memory. He whispered to himself, "Nanny for Queen."

"We don't take any play money here. Only Albion credits or Tejas currency."

"What about this?" Desmond produced a gold coin. "Surely you could make do with this."

"We don't make change." The man held the coin between his index finger and thumb with an appraising gaze. "But this will guarantee . . . two nights."

"Three."

"Fine, but no refunds if you opt to leave early."

Movement caught Desmond's eye in the mirror behind the man. He hadn't put the habits of spycraft behind him. Shrouded among the winding stairs, a sheet-covered coat rack, and some decorative plants, a figure stood near the back corner of the lobby under the stairwell. His high black boots and dark pants didn't draw attention to him. However, his cape reminded Desmond of someone. A Kabbalist agent. Desmond whirled around, brandishing his cane like a sword. The man wasn't there.

"Everything all right?" the concierge asked.

"Yes it's fine." Desmond glanced from one end of the

lobby to the other. Finding no trace of the man, he lowered his cane. "I thought I saw an old . . . friend."

The concierge eyed the cane. "We don't look too kindly on those sorts of friendships rekindling their acquaintance. This is a much gentler joint than the Redeemer, I promise you."

"I'm dining there this evening. With Mr. Hearst." Desmond let the name fall to see what kind of reaction it would receive.

"My, you *do* have fancy friends." The man handed him a set of keys without further commentary.

Desmond filled a water basin and washed his face. He'd drawn a bath for Lij and let the boy splash around while he finished donning his attire for the evening. If there was one thing he truly missed of his old life, it was his dandied wardrobe. Theirs was a life on the run, but he still allowed himself one clothing indulgence. A fuchsia-colored shirt against a dark emerald suit. A pocket kerchief matched his shirt.

"How do you like the room?" Desmond asked as Lij emerged from the bathroom.

"It is fine, I guess."

"What do you mean when you say 'I guess'?"

"I'm guessing. Isn't that what I'm supposed to say?" Lij didn't look at him.

"Are you enjoying being around people a little more?"

"One percent. I hear all the noise." Lij wore white pinstriped pants and a collared blue shirt with large pockets. Lij loved pockets.

"Well, let's see what the good people of Abandon have to offer."

Desmond helped him finish dressing before putting the final trimmings on his own outfit. He eased an unlit pipe into his mouth and grabbed his tan-handled cane. His dark sunglasses hid a third of his face.

Marveling at the mechanical horses as they trotted along, Desmond hadn't seen such craftsmanship since leaving Jamaica. Hundreds of metal squares, like armor weave-molded on a frame, formed their gleaming, sleek bodies. The clockwork beasts threw chunks of mud with each step. Only a few horse-drawn carriages filled the streets. Unlike other cities, where cars clogged the paved city arteries with such thick congestion that every morning, the city suffered a traffic coronary.

"Everyone here seems to have a gun," Lij said.

"They do love their guns here."

"I don't like them. They hurt people."

"That's what they were designed to do," Desmond said.

"You hurt people."

"Sometimes. That was what I was trained to do in order to protect the people I cared about."

"This one time, you hurt a man in a cape."

"I remember."

"He came after us. He kept following us from place to place, like a shadow. He said he was after me and that I was a weapon."

"You're not a weapon."

"He lied and said I was. I didn't like him. He made me..." Lij clapped his hands. Every now and then, Lij would get stuck on a point. Like a needle caught in the groove of a phonogram, he kept coming back to whatever made him anxious until he worked it out of his system.

"How did he make you feel?" Desmond held his hand loosely but gave it a reassuring squeeze.

"Scared. And angry. I wanted to go to my quiet place."

"The special room?"

"No, my quiet place. They sometimes let me do that. It helped me get calm."

"We all sometimes need to go to our quiet place."

"Yours is under a tree."

Desmond smiled. "It helps me think."

"This one time you ran and jumped on a man with a cape. You started kicking and punching and rolling on the ground."

"I remember. Maybe we shouldn't talk about it."

"All right." Lij walked a little more.

A man limped by on a set of crutches, his leg missing from the knee down. Two men punched each other while a crowd watched. Neither one particularly angry, their fight seemed more of an exercise in venting anger. A trashcan fire warmed a family between buildings. Rats scurried along the windowsill of the closed general store, anxious to get to the feed inventory. What Desmond hated most was the smell. The mud may have been mixed with waste from sewer overflows. A heavy odor fell from the factory. Everything had a hint of something burnt, as if someone overworked the bellows and stoked flames, scorching the walls of buildings.

Lij snapped back to attention. "You kept kicking and punching him. I thought I was in trouble."

"You weren't in trouble."

"I thought I made trouble."

"It wasn't your fault. Bad men wanted to do bad things to you."

"And you kept kicking and punching him. You kept me safe."

"I told you, I protect the people I care about."

"I don't like this place. There are too many shadows."

"I know." Desmond knew they were being watched. Herded. Each step toward the Redeemer carried a sense of inevitability. If their enemies had found them, best to gather them, have them reveal themselves. Deal with them one way or another.

A thin haze of smoky air hung in the air as if not wanting to cross the threshold of the Redeemer's lobby. In the flickering gaslit glow of the chandelier, a few men sat around card tables, smoking pipes and muttering to themselves. They held their cards either close to their vests or flat against the table. A series of open flames ringed the small stage. A piano player let his fingers dance along the keys, producing a jaunty melody. But no showgirls took to the stage. The music rose and fell, a choreographed metronome. A few men glanced with expectation to the stage, but without so much as a curtain rustle to hold their attention, they turned back to their games.

Stepping inside, he felt all eyes in the room quickly fall on him. The piano ceased its tinkling, holding its breath in an extended pause before picking back up a few measures later. Desmond scanned the saloon, but he didn't see their erstwhile dinner companion.

"This here's no place for a child, boy."

Desmond fully expected to turn and see the rude man from earlier that day. Though this new man could have been his relation, it was not him. Desmond began to wonder if there were but two sorts of people in Tejas:

the rude ones itching for a confrontation and the overly chatty ones looking to learn a stranger's life story. He didn't like the way the man looked at either of them. "There are no children here."

The man took a moment to size Desmond up one last time. Through the thick lenses of his beer goggles, he saw something he didn't like. Or he'd sobered up enough for common sense to take over. "Just giving you fair warning's all."

The man stumbled back toward the saloon, the darkness and smoky haze swallowing him in a few steps. Desmond turned in time to see the woman from the street stride through the doorway.

"Well, ain't this a pig living in muck," she said.

"I'm getting accustomed to the constant posturing, I suppose," Desmond said.

"You certainly clean up nice."

"It's not every day one is invited to dine with the closest thing to a Chancellor of a city one had never been in before."

"When you put it that way, I'm downright envious."

"Well, I'm curious as to what he has to say. At the very least, it's a free meal and I expect it to be interesting."

"Interesting . . . is a word." She stared at him with a gaze that struck him as one part flirtation and two parts appraisal.

"Well, well, well, look at all the pretty people gathered in one place. I doubt the Redeemer can take it." Mr. Hearst paraded down the steps, taking his time to ensure all eyes remained on him. He capped his green outfit with a cowboy hat, but he wore it like he was new to it and it didn't fit natural. When he reached the bottom of the stairwell, he studied the woman and Desmond. The intensity of scrutiny reminded Desmond of how Lij often stared at people who drew his full attention. "I hope I'm not intruding."

"Not at all. We didn't see you and we thought it best to wait by the main door," Desmond said.

"Yeah, the Redeemer's not exactly casual family dining, but it'll do in a pinch. I'm here now; shall we go in?" Mr. Hearst held the door, then ran his eyes up and down the woman. "Where are my manners? Garrison Hearst at your service."

"Cayt Siringo."

"Enchanted." Mr. Hearst bent low to kiss her hand. "You, my dear, are welcome to join us."

"Now, I wouldn't want to intrude," Cayt said.

"Nonsense. I'd be kicking myself for the rest of the night if I refused the opportunity for the company of so exquisite a creature."

"In that case, I'd love to join you." Cayt curtsied and stepped through the doorway.

Eyes from each of the tables watched them to their seats, some more surreptitiously than others. The rude man and the one who could be his relation kept their eyes on the drinks in front of them. A waitress met them immediately and ushered them to the rear of the saloon. Another set of stairs wrapped around the back wall and side of the room, creating a small alcove around a back table. It afforded them a view of the entire saloon floor as well as a measure of privacy.

The waitress cast an uncertain eye toward Lij, but Mr. Hearst waved off her unneeded attention. Desmond moved to the seat closest to the back wall and immediately noted the exits. Though he left the seat beside him vacant, Lij refused it and stood behind him.

"Cigarette?" Mr. Hearst held out a gold cigarette container. "Carolina-grown."

"Don't mind if I do." Cayt took a cigarette and held it to her lips for Mr. Hearst to light.

"And you?"

"I have my own." Desmond reached into his vest pocket to withdraw the pouch. He deftly rolled a spliff only half of what he normally rolled, so that he'd have enough to roll one last one later. With quite the production, he took a long hit, held the smoke for several heartbeats before letting loose a thick cloud of smoke.

"An unusual odor, I must say," Mr. Hearst said.

"It's not from Carolina."

"Speaking of unusual, so is your accent. Where are you from?"

"You're the second person to remark on my accent." Desmond smirked at Cayt.

"I may have mentioned that if he were affecting an Albion accent, or worse, a Tejan one, he still had room to perfect it," Cayt said.

"I must say I do agree with the lady. Still, I can't quite place it," Mr. Hearst pressed.

"Jamaica." Desmond smiled to keep up pretenses, but he knew an interrogation when he heard one. He'd dealt with men like Mr. Hearst before. Men who enjoyed their power but enjoyed watching people dance to their tune even more.

"You're a long way from home."

"We're on an extended vacation. When I was young, I always wished to see more of the world. To better know its people, walk among them. Learn from them."

"How much of the world do you plan to see?"

The man fished for information. Desmond wasn't going to give him much. "We haven't decided. There's so much to see here."

"We're so close to the Five Civilized Tribes border; had you given that any consideration?"

"It was difficult enough crossing the Tejas border

from Albion. The borders of the Five Civilized Tribes seem particularly . . . contested."

"You know how border disputes go." Mr. Hearst waved his cigarette about in search of an ashtray. A waitress brought one over and then busied herself at another table. "Folks squabbling over who owns what land."

"Land ownership is where true wealth lies," Desmond said.

"And the resources they represent. Some of the California lands have gold veins so thick that you can scoop up with your hands . . . all going to waste 'cause these godless, bloodthirsty heathens ain't got the sense God gave them."

"I'm quite familiar with being seen as a potential well of resources. It's Albion's chief lesson of interaction with its neighbors."

Mr. Hearst read Desmond's expression of unease. "I don't mean to offend. Look here, I've got nothing against those people. I just have a habit of saying what a lot of people think, especially around these parts, and—not being politically shrewd—I forget my words may shock some folks. If it makes you feel any better, you should know that I'm part Indian. On my father's side."

"You're part full of shit," Cayt said. "Everyone claims they're part Indian, like it's some sort of fashion statement."

Mr. Hearst took the casual insult in stride, but he slowly turned to her like a missile turret acquiring a new target. "So, how is it that you and Mr. Coke became acquainted?"

"An accident of circumstances, I'd say," Cayt said.

"We bumped into each other on the promenade. Not too long after you and I were first introduced," Desmond said.

"It was a busy day for you. Lots of interesting characters to meet," Mr. Hearst said.

"The people of Tejas do love to . . . introduce themselves. It's not how I imagined this place would be."

"You think us all gun-crazed militia types, barricading ourselves in our homes with stores of food and ammo, waiting for the government invasion?"

"So the news would have people believe."

"The *Vox Dei* and *Vox Populi* are owned by Lord Leighton Melbourne. The *Vox Populi* electro-transmissions are an opiate for the masses, and I'd sooner wipe my ass with the *Vox Dei* than read it."

Desmond shifted. "There's a lady and child present."

"Well, how a man tends to the needs of his ass says a lot about him," Cayt said.

"I like this one. She's a hoot. Can I buy you all a round of drinks before we get down to it? I have it on good authority that the bartender keeps a bottle of thirty-three-year-old whiskey from the Scottish highlands in his special stock. I've been hankering to try it."

"Nothing for me, thank you," Desmond said.

"Not a drinking man?"

"Not as much these days."

"The duty of parenthood, I suppose." Mr. Hearst snapped his fingers and the waitress stepped to attention. "I never hope to find out."

"Whiskey. Neat," Cayt said.

"Two sarsaparillas for the gentleman and his son. Two whiskeys. The good stuff. Neat." Mr. Hearst waved her off like he brushed lint from his shoulders. "Now, you were saying about how you two met."

"Up until a couple hours ago, we'd never met," Cayt said again.

"Cayt—may I call you Cayt?"

"Of course. We're all friends here."

"Cayt, how does it that a young woman such as yourself finds her way to the fair city of Abandon?"

"Whatever do you mean?"

"I mean, despite how Desmond portrays our international appeal, we're fairly off the beaten track."

"You're here," she said.

"I happen to own a residence here to oversee some of my interests, but, to be frank, most folks find this here town to be like a wart on a gentleman's unmentionables.

No one finds their way here on accident."

"I'd say the tent city on the outskirts begs to differ."

"Those are drifters and migrant workers. Folks like Mr. Coke here, looking for work as they pass through."

"And I couldn't be?" Cayt asked.

"Don't be so modest." Mr. Hearst stirred. He leaned forward, his eyes intense. His voice dropped a little with the vague hint of patience running out.

"I'm a girl of gossamer interests."

"What does that mean?"

"I come and go as I please." Cayt met his eyes, unblinking. She reached into her purse. Mr. Hearst hard-eyed her movements but relaxed when she withdrew her fan.

"A leaf blown in the wind," Mr. Hearst said.

"Exactly."

"A woman of independent means? I'm not familiar with the Siringo family name."

"We're . . . I'm from Matagorda State. In southwestern Tejas."

"I thought I recognized that particular brand of twang. Living off the family trust?"

"Manners." Cayt unfurled her fan and began to flutter it. She upticked her chin toward the boy. "I almost died when I was his age. Smallpox. My mother passed away soon after. I learned early on how to make my own way."

"What work brings you to Abandon?"

Desmond turned to her to take particular note of how she'd respond to this line of inquiry.

Cayt passed the briefest of glances between them. Her lips upturned slightly at the edges, enjoying an unspoken game. "I'm strictly a consultant. I take on jobs that intrigue me."

"A woman of intrigue. How did you get into . . . consulting?" Mr. Hearst asked.

"You know how you get to that age when you find yourself rather adrift in life? Folks didn't think I was going to make it, especially since I was a scrawny something. When I got better, I was determined to be a cowgirl. I was a crack shot and pretty fair with a rope. Then I bumped into a phrenologist at a county fair. He took a reading of my cranium and convinced me to change my line of work." Cayt closed her fan. "I might ask you the question of why do you take such an interest in us."

"You two are what I call anomalies."

"How so?"

"Neither of you quite fit. You're like a tick bite that I can't seem to scratch. A couple of strangers who blow into town about the same time. You may know each other already, you may not. It might all be coincidence, but I'm not a big believer in coincidence."

"A place like Abandon, off the beaten track as you say, would be the perfect place for someone to make a fresh start for themselves," Desmond said with caution. "Away from interference from the crown."

"A place for a feller . . . or lady . . . to get lost," Cayt said.

"Or to be found." Mr. Hearst settled back into his chair.

The waitress arrived with the drinks. She poured out the bottles of sarsaparilla into tall glasses and left the remainder in the bottles besides them. She set the two shot glasses in front of both Mr. Hearst and Cayt. Everyone eyed their drinks. The air between them slowly soured as their patience with the game were thin for them all now.

"To good health," Mr. Hearst raised a shot glass.

Cayt raised her glass, clinked it against his, and then downed her drink in a single gulp. She overturned the empty glass and slammed it to the table. "Sipping is for a lady's tea party."

Mr. Hearst tossed his drink back and slammed his glass to the table. He shook two fingers at the waitress before turning back to Desmond. "It's not too often that we get a Negro passing through here."

The man delivered the words like a probe, waiting to see how Desmond would react.

"It's a free republic, as I understand." Desmond sipped his sarsaparilla.

"The freest." Mr. Hearst threw his head back with a relaxed chuckle. "That damn fool regent, Lincoln, did his level best to tear the country apart way back when until the crown saw fit to have him removed."

"A conspiracy buff?" Cayt asked.

"A realist. Regent Lincoln was bad for business. And this here United States territory is the engine that drives the business of Albion. We can trace the Tejas Free Republic and the current tensions directly back to his original missteps."

"Sounds like given Tejas's independent status, you ought to be more grateful to him, then." Desmond hoped that he disguised his bristling at any disparagement of Regent Lincoln and what he attempted to do. With his efforts to free a people, in Jamaica, he was hailed as a hope for a new era of relations between the two countries.

"I am but a simple businessman with several business interests. As my reputation is largely the stuff of dime novels, I'll admit that some of my family's fortune found its origins in smuggling, bootlegging, and piracy before we fully legitimized and headed west. I followed the railways and airships, like a hopper, except my goal was to control them, not hitch rides on them. And when I found Abandon, I found my home. Well, my base of operations hidden from all things civilized. It was here that I established my consortium of like-minded businessmen."

Desmond took another swig of his sarsaparilla. The saloon patrons chatted amiably in low murmurs. None of them ordered any drinks. No one touched their cards. Too many cast surreptitious glances toward their table. "Kabbalists."

"It has taken on the appearance of a quasi-political movement. At its heart, it is about people pursuing truths. About themselves. About mankind. About the universal forces that govern our lives." Mr. Hearst took another cigarette for himself. "Politics is always a tricky business to discuss in polite company."

"I hope you don't hold back on my account," Cayt said.

"All right, then, the take-home lesson is that people always get the government they allow. Albion officials telling us we're trespassing on our own land. Here in Tejas, we got sick and tired of the crown creeping into our everyday lives. No matter what you're doing, there the crown is with a law and a tax. We just want to be left alone. The tensions you referred to began with our protests over the crown declaring ownership of public lands. Land seized for their mineral reserves. That was the final straw. It didn't take much to stir up some anti-crown sentiment. Albion rules with a heavy hand, too much control, too much interference in lives and businesses. We were already frustrated with the crown over their oppressive laws and regulation. Taxation without representation. All of their oppressive tactics. Dissidents had been fleeing to Tejas in such droves, the phrase 'Gone to Tejas' became popular.

"Our little . . . insurrection party threw a cog into Albion's Western Design dream: a coast-to-coast version of the United States, and they've resented us ever since. The crown can label us occupiers all they want. Our armed citizens patrols our borders as members of the Watchmen. Our militia men stand as our first line of armed resistance against government tyranny."

"You protect what's yours," Desmond said.

Mr. Hearst leveled a cool eye at him; his gaze flicked behind him to Lij. He downed the second shot of whiskey and slammed the empty glass on the table. "Doesn't that boy ever speak?"

"All the time. To me. When he feels safe." Desmond regripped the handle of his cane.

"I grow weary of these games. Let us get down to the business at hand."

"And what business is that?" Cayt asked.

"I assume the same business that brought you to Abandon, Miss Siringo. Shall I tell you a story?"

"I do so enjoy a good yarn."

"In Jamaica, there was a Maroon leader named Colonel Malcolm Juba. Malcolm the First, he declared himself, a petty tyrant of a man, unreasonable and generally a misanthrope when it comes to business, but no one could say that he lacked vision. Or audacity. Though he ruled his kingdom with a cruel hand, he could not stem the raucous tide of people whose interests collided. None were strong enough to overthrow him, but their constant agitation made his rule troublesome. He constantly had to deal with threats within his kingdom.

"No outsider could be at all certain about the internal politics of the Jamaican power structure. The Rastafarians had their own factions. Obeahists worked 'The Science,' mixing their brand of mysticism and politics. There was even this group of radicals who called themselves the *Niyabingi*. They fancied themselves secret soldiers who carried out the will of the people. They planned to ride the world of the Colonel and allow the people to remake their government.

"All of the various interests vied for the power or minds of the people. So Malcolm decided that he needed a symbol, a story to stir the imaginations and unite the hearts of his people. A living idea he could control as well as exploit. If he could not find a symbol, he would make one. He thought back through the history of his people and chose their most personal story. The Rastafarians had a leader, Haile Selassie, the Roaring Lion, who fit the bill. We have to be careful because names have power." He tried to guess an answer from Lij's face, but none was forthcoming. "Born Tafari Makonnen, the King of Abyssinia, a messiah descended from King Solomon and the Queen of Sheba.

"Malcolm turned to the science of the Age of Reason. From a sample of His Imperial Majesty, his scientists played with cells, the building blocks of life, to create new life in a glass womb. Without mother. Without father. Only Malcolm. The plan was to raise the boy as the returned Haile Selassie, with Malcolm as the man behind the curtain. But he didn't count on a member of the *Niyabingi* going off script and taking the boy out of play entirely. Stirred up quite the hornet's nest."

"As you said, people get the government they allow," Desmond said.

"I don't like that story," Lij whispered in his ear. "And there are a lot of shadows in here."

"I noticed." Desmond had that feeling again of being watched. Stalked. His hunters remained out of sight, though he knew they were there. Like mirages noticed only out of the corners of his eyes.

"If I may, I'd like to propose a peaceable solution to our little impasse," Mr. Hearst said with the smugness of a man hiding an ace up his sleeve at the card table. "What if war was declared, everyone showed up, but no one fought? Not Albion, not Jamaica, not Tejas."

"Like a standoff?" Desmond frowned skeptically.

"No winners. Well, except for the people who designed and sold their weapons."

"And the people in charge of rebuilding afterwards," Cayt added.

"And the gravediggers," Desmond said. "There is always big business in death."

"We are on the cusp of a new age. A technology race to the next breakthrough. He who controls the technology controls the future. And Lij *is* technology." Mr. Hearst rested both arms on the table and huddled toward them. He continued in a conspiratorial stage whisper. "I have my agents placed about this room. All of them watching and waiting for my signal."

"I know. They're sloppy. I spotted them when we arrived at the Fountain. I imagine a couple are going through our room as we chat."

"You imagine correctly."

"What about Cayt?"

"What makes you think I couldn't handle myself?" Cayt asked.

"Oh, I suspect you can. My guess is that you're a special operative with the Pinkerton Agency," Desmond said. "And that was your partner Mr. Hearst or the good citizens of Abandon left on display."

"I wondered," Mr. Hearst said. "For whom do you . . . consult?"

"I wouldn't be much of a consultant if I just gave up that sort of information, now, would I?" she said.

"I have my suspicions. Lord Melbourne would have great interest in the secrets the boy carries within him. So, the ways I see it, you ain't got but a couple of choices. You see, you ain't as lost as you thought you were. I know you're here. Lord Melbourne knows you're here. I'm guessing your own people were on the next airship out of Jamaica and can't be far behind. So, either you make your deal with the devil of your choosing or you make peace with whatever god you people pray to these days." Mr. Hearst pushed away from the table slightly, like a man stuffed after a full meal. He surveyed his guests one more time. "I'll leave you two to discuss your options among yourselves. You can reach me in my suite with your answer."

Cayt put her hand on his, halting him. "Before you go, I have a couple of observations."

"And what might those be, little lady?" Mr. Hearst asked.

"The first is strictly conjecture. The name Garrison Hearst carries with it a significant weight. He is a man of note, used to dealing with captains of industry, regents, even royalty. I have trouble believing that he would, in person, have a face-to-face meeting that a low-level aide-de-camp; am I saying that right?" She turned to Desmond, who half-shrugged. "That an aide-de-camp should handle."

"Are you saying that I'm not who I represent myself to be?"

"Oh, I believe who you represent, only that you aren't him. Second." She turned to Desmond. "How many do you count?"

Without missing a beat, Desmond noted the positions of the other patrons and the bartender. "A dozen."

"A dozen of your men stand between us and the front door. I have trouble believing that you're just going to let us walk out of here, no matter what we decide."

"How you leave here is entirely up to you." For the first time, Mr. Hearst's voice wavered.

Cayt patted Mr. Hearst down while keeping a friendly smile on her face. "Whether you live longer than the next few minutes so that you can give Mr. Hearst our answer depends on you keeping your hands in plain sight and you remaining all friendly-like."

They sat in silence. The moment stretched. Two men blocked the main door. The ones playing poker hadn't overturned a card in quite a while. It was like they were too bored to keep up the pretense while waiting for a signal. Mr. Hearst's exit was probably their sign. Now they grew anxious.

"Do you still have the music box?" Lij asked.

Mr. Hearst jumped at the sound of the boy's voice.

"I sure do, hon." Cayt retrieved the box and handed

it to him. "You can keep it."

The opening notes of "Beautiful Dreamer" tinkled from the metal tines as the clockwork gears spun the tiny porcelain dancer.

"You want him for your employer," Desmond said.

"The only thing I want right now is to make it out of this room alive. You saw what they did to my partner."

"If they are armed like the last agent who attacked us, their weapons are probably set to stun in order to not to risk hurting the boy."

"Mine aren't," she said. "Besides, they might be hesitant to fire with their ringleader here with us."

"Are you even armed?"

"A lady never tells. You?"

"Swords don't have stun settings." Desmond slowly turned the handle of his cane and withdrew his blade underneath the table.

"You seriously brought a sword to a gunfight?"

"I held out hope that all I'd have to fight tonight was an overdone steak."

The weight of a person creeping down the stairwell caused a step above them to creak. With the flick of her wrists, twin modified Colt Mustangs slid into Cayt's hands along mechanical arm braces hidden by her dangling sleeves. She fired twice above them and a body tumbled over the bannister. Desmond overturned their table.

"Thirteen, then," he said.

The men in the saloon scrambled for cover and began to fire. The air sizzled. Electric pulses from handheld weapons battered the overturned table. Desmond stretched his neck to the left, then to the right, slowly popping his joints. He glanced from Cayt's drawn weapons to her eyes. She gazed from his sword back to his eyes. With a nod, they established the barest of truces.

Cayt dove. Sliding from behind the table, she fired from her side. Two men yelped in response.

Desmond lunged toward the nearest table. The rude man took cover behind a wooden pole near his table. Desmond leapt at him before he could fire. With his free hand, Desmond took him by the hair and slammed his head into the table. Desmond kept moving. The man who could have been kin to the rude one fumbled in bringing his weapon to bear. Desmond rammed the hilt of his cane into the side of the man's skull.

I guess there's a stun setting after all, he thought.

Desmond whirled to scoop up Lij and make a break for the door. When he turned, a man clutched the boy to him. His weapon trained at Lij's head.

The man started to speak. "Now, you just . . ."

A weapon fired. The man's face grew quizzical, as if not understanding what happened. A neat hole perforated his forehead. His eyes rolled skyward and his body dropped where it stood. Desmond turned and nodded. Cayt returned the gesture.

She leapt and ran along the bar, firing her weapons madly. Yet she hit targets with a preternatural ease. Four more bodies dropped. When she ran out of bullets, Cayt flung the guns as distraction. She laughed wildly as she pounced on several men.

With Lij in tow behind him, Desmond wasted few movements. A man aimed a shotgun at Desmond's head. Stepping toward the man, Desmond knocked the weapon to the side like he was blocking a punch. He ran the man through with his blade. There was a wet *chuff* and the man let loose a soft grunt. Desmond withdrew the blade and moved toward the door.

Four men in black capes ran into the room to join the two men guarding the door. The ponchos unfurled, revealing the mechanical works of their lower torsos. Gears whirred around a central cavity, which housed a series of electrodes. Electricity arced between them. Kabbalist agents. The men formed a semicircle.

Cayt tumbled into them like a four-limbed bowling ball. From the corner of his eye, he caught her kicking a man. She sent him headfirst into the corner of the bar. A punch sent another man sprawling. She grabbed a mug from the bar, shattering it against the head of one man, she jammed the handle of what remained into the chest cavity of another.

Desmond grabbed the nearest man. He spun him around to use as a shield against the remaining men. In formation, the men moved like armored vehicles. An agent threw a slow, telegraphed blow. As a squad, they depended too much on their armor to absorb much of the punishment. Desmond sidestepped the blow. He jammed his sword into the gears of the man's arm. This severed the limb at the shoulder.

Desmond blocked two punches with the sheath of his cane. He thrust it into the man's gut. Desmond dropped to one knee and spun. His blade sliced across the man's legs. It clanged, metal on metal. He rolled before the man stomped where Desmond's head once was. Scrabbling to his feet, Desmond barely managed to avoid a punch. He turned to his left and ducked. He hooked his cane handle to the man's ankle. Sweeping his feet out from under him, Desmond cracked the man in the head as he fell.

Cayt slid under a wild punch, pivoted, and slammed her elbow into a man's groin. Twice for good measure. The man dropped his weapon. She head-butted him and let him drop to the ground.

Lij stood near the door, between Desmond and Cayt. "Beautiful Dancer" played like a mechanical flute.

"We have unfinished business, you and I." Cayt took in ragged gasps of air.

"How so?" Desmond breathed heavily, taking a slow step away from the pile of men.

"You need to hand the boy over to me."

"The boy is my charge."

"And I have an employer to report to." Cayt held out her arm. No weapon sprang to her hand. She hunted for a pulse weapon.

Desmond grabbed Lij with such force, the boy dropped his music box. A low wail grew to a mad howl as Lij kicked and screamed. Dashing through the saloon lobby, Desmond ran with the boy under his arm to the street. A mechanical horse was parked at the curb. He slung the keening boy on top of the horse, pressing him hard—he was afraid, too hard—into the horse's nape for fear the lad in his fit would wriggle free and fall off. With a yell, Desmond spun the horse into action.

Cayt ran onto the street and fired once after them.

Desmond's side burned, but he couldn't chance checking his wound until they got free of Tejas' borders. With their enemies pressing in on them, they had to keep moving to make it into the Five Civilized Tribes territory.

III.

Fire

BLOOD PUDDLED at Desmond Coke's feet, creating clumps of ruddy mud. He'd opened his wound again. The ache in his side reduced to a dull throb, he braced himself against the outcrop of exposed tree roots, his pulse gun drawn. Pressed into the makeshift hutch, his breath issued in thick plumes on the unusually frigid air. Palming the modified Colt Mustang with both hands to secure his blood-slickened grasp, the gun grip fit into his palm like a smooth stone. Palming it during the melee at the Redeemer, he never trusted the weapon, but he realized its necessity. He even managed to acquire a new charge pack for it. He preferred his sword, but that was back at the camp. Desmond lowered his head and closed his eyes, straining his ears, knowing he'd hear nothing. He chanced a peek above the ridge. He swore shadows skulked among the tree line, drawing nearer to his position moving through the woods, little more than a determined breeze barely rustling leaves in their passing.

Searching for him and the boy.

The air thickened with the threat of another incoming storm, redolent with the cloying smell of budding trees. The nearby creek swelled high along its bank, full due to all the recent rain. Its harsh susurrus joined the chorus of night sounds. Birds called to one another and the trees thrummed with the calls of cicadas. The gentle breeze picked up, deepening the chill and flecking the occasional drop of rain from overhanging leaves onto him. Desmond turned up the collar on his jacket. A voice echoed among the trees. No, not among the trees: in his mind. Perhaps. Low and raspy, something just north of sultry yet with the steel edge of mocking to it.

"You have something my employer wants," Cayt said.

"Someone," Desmond corrected, not sure if he spoke the words or thought them.

"People. Minerals. Technology. Everything is a resource. The more scarce the resource, the more value it has to those who wish to control them."

"And you are no more than your master's mawga *foot lapdog."*

"Maybe so. Tell me how much you enjoy my bite."

Pain sliced through his side with the exertion. The reopened wound nagged at his muscles, taunting his every movement. He feared infection. With the air temperature dropping, the cold cut deep to his marrow. Long used to the warm Jamaican sun, his blood ran thin. The bleak winter had been long and hard and he thought he might never know warmth again.

Through the brush, the raised tracks of the maglev train snaked through the woods. His ears had popped the last time a train sped through. He could only guess its speed as it wound its way through the Five Civilized Tribes' main cities. The nation spread all along the West Coast of the continent. Sure-footed as a goat, Desmond climbed down the embankment along a path he traversed. He crouched low at the sudden crunch of leaves. He held his breath, hoping that a falling branch caused the sound. Brushing aside the still-bare branches, he spotted them long before he heard their tell-tale mechan ical whirl.

A mechanical beast approximating the shape of a wolf stalked through the trees. When the moon peeked from behind its cloud cover, Desmond managed to make out two other similar shapes in the patrol pack. Pairs of red eyes peered in his direction. Pushing his back against the thick tree trunk, he shielded himself from their photo-electric stare. He timed the interval between their patrols and was thankful for the increased cover spring leaves would bring to help hide them from the view of the mechanical eagles which soared by day. Still, the pattern of the patrol had changed, bringing them too near to their camp. In the morning, he and the boy would have to make their way farther along the river. Perhaps they might make their way into Canada within the month, and maybe then he might feel a little bit safer.

Desmond limped back to the camp. His time as a member of the *Niyabingi* had prepared him well, just as his training allowed him to mask his pain. It would only worry the boy to see him hobbling about. He foraged for wood that would burn without smoke. Again, as he approached the camp, Desmond made enough noise to avoid startling the boy.

Lij barely turned his head in Desmond's direction, as if noting him from the corner of his eye was all the acknowledgement needed. Never the chattiest of children to begin with, Lij had become more withdrawn in recent weeks. Much longer on the run and Desmond feared he might lose him altogether. Constantly retreating to his thoughts, Lij's mind slowly collapsed under its own gravity, from which he rarely escaped. He wore a simple drop-shouldered collarless white shirt under a soot-colored sack coat and matching hat. Looking at his mud-smudged face, Desmond was reminded how young the boy was.

Desmond had become alert to the fact that they were the prey to some unseen hunter when they trekked through northern Tejas. They had rented a room at a hotel on the seedier side of Amarillo, both to disappear among the ranks of the poor and forgotten and because everywhere else they had traveled, they stuck out too much. Ever the *obroni,* the outsider, as his people called him. A Jamaican in a grey, single-breasted pinstripe suit, its full jacket draping down to his knees. A light red shirt, mostly hidden by a yellow cross-hatched vest, topped with a green bow tie. And he was still too brown, with too much accent.

In retrospect, he might as well have painted a bull's-eye on the pair of them.

They left Tejas with a much lighter pack and a wardrobe more appropriate for their travels. Desmond still favored wearing a suit, but it was coal-colored, with no flamboyant shading to his shirt nor pocket square. The suit had not been spared in their march through the woods. Mud smeared the underside of his sleeve and he didn't want to contemplate the source of the greasy stain along his pants. His black trilby hat perched at an odd angle on his head, yet he stopped to pick free a stray thread from his cuff.

Heading into the territory of the Five Civilized Tribes was a dangerous-enough gambit, but they'd crossed over the contested California border without incident. Despite the day's newspaper proclaiming Regent Clinton's latest dalliances, the expansion engine of Albion marched inexorably forward. Not content with their portion of the American colony, the Albion Empire had its hands full: flexing its muscle in an attempt to rattle rival power Jamaica; disputes with Tejas; and distracted by their attempts to compromise the aboriginal people's border. Albion's forces were more focused on those who might attempt to sneak out rather than in.

Desmond tended to the campfire to keep it low. He would murder a small village to roll a spliff. But chiba leaves were in short supply these days, and he had more urgent needs rather than draw further attention to them with his inquiries: he needed to close the wound in his side. His mother had taught him to sew a long time before, and though he'd forgotten the finer points of technique, he could make do with a needle and thread. Without those at his disposal, he opted for a cruder measure. Withdrawing the blade hidden within his cane, he placed it in the fire.

"*Raasclaat!*" he cursed when he pressed the heated metal against his wound.

"*Raasclaat,*" Lij echoed.

Desmond paused for a moment, then burst out laughing, a dark, hiccupping shudder over his pain. The boy turned to him with a curious expression like he was trying to identify an insect he'd never seen before. "No, Lij. You shouldn't say that. It's not . . . appropriate."

The boy turned back to the bobbing flickers. Desmond fixed them a simple stew of game meat and ate it with biscuits he'd picked up from the last town they'd passed through. Desmond longed for a plate of ackee and saltfish. He'd never truly developed a taste for it when Lij's age. He'd hated the way the heavy aroma filled his house when his mother fixed it every Saturday morning. But nothing would taste more like home, would nurse the true parts of his soul, like a plate of it right now.

"Home," Lij said without preamble. The word came so sudden and unexpected, it somewhat alarmed Desmond.

"You want to go home?"

"Home."

"I'm not sure I understand what you mean. We have to keep moving if I'm going to keep you safe. . . ." Desmond's voice trailed off with the realization that this was their life now: never settling down, always on the move. Sweat beaded Desmond's forehead, his skin flushed with fever. Checking his wound for striation, he feared he might be succumbing to infection. If chills set in, he would be in serious trouble. He had been on excursions in worse conditions during his time as a member of the *Niyabingi,* but the boy shivered, despite being so close to the fire. This was no life for a child. Even one as special as Lij.

"Can you tell me a story?" Lij asked. A ring of command hinted at the edge of the boy's voice.

"We Jamaicans are some of the best storytellers on the planet." Desmond smiled broadly, allowing the rare glimpse of the full whites of his teeth. "Stories are our cultural inheritance, passed down, parent to child, connecting us to our past." The boy said nothing but stared absently into the fires as if calculating the mathematical rhythms of the flames' dance. Perhaps what they both needed was somethng with the familiar ring of home to it. Desmond cleared his throat.

"Each of the great rivers of Jamaica were guarded by water spirits known as the River Mumma. Some people say that they protected the source of those rivers. In the sun, they looked like the most beautiful of women, their long black hair falling down across their bare bodies. From the waist down, they had the body of a large fish. Few dared to anger a River Mumma, not even risking to fish near where one might rest. The fish of that river were thought to be her children, so no one ate them. Some people whispered that if the River Mumma was captured, the river would dry up. And if you ever met a River Mumma's eyes, then dog nyam yuh suppa!

Desmond found himself imitating his mother's voice and cadence as he slipped into Jamaican patois. He'd been very conscious of not speaking in patois around Lij. The old lessons of language were hard to unlearn and be free of. It had long been drilled into him that patois was spoken by the common people. Proper English was the language spoken by and to outsiders. Maroon, true descendants of the Ashanti people, spoke Asante-Twi with each other. Neither he nor Lij were truly Maroon, though raised among them. They were *obroni* who only had each other. Nearly lost in the telling of the story, he paused to see if he still held what passed for Lij's attention.

Lij's eyes flicked from the fire to Desmond, back to the flames: the man's cue to continue.

In days gone by, people would go to the river at sacred times and make sacrifices to her when they wanted to cross the river she guarded. They would come and dance myal *for her, but you don't know about that.* Myal *was deep magic, the dance that called on our ancestors. And they brought food for the River Mumma.*

"Why?" Lij asked without turning to Desmond.

"Because the River Mumma were the guardians of secrets and secrets, like mysteries, were to be respected.

There came a time when a great drought fell upon the land. The workers at a sugar estate persuaded the owner to sacrifice an ox to the River Mumma so that she would cause it to rain. The owner had little use for his workers "superstitious nonsense," but curiosity arose in him and he wanted to see this guardian for himself. If she were as powerful as they claimed, then perhaps the secrets she protected would also be of great value.

So the owner followed his workers to the great rock where the River Mumma rested. The noonday sun crawled across the sky. From a distance, he saw a figure reclining, combing her long black hair. At the sound of his approach, she turned and their eyes met, but only for an instant. She disappeared. When the owner reached the spot where she once sat, the only thing remaining was her long, gold comb. Then he caught a flash out the corner of his eye.

The owner turned to the waters. Something bobbed just beneath the surface. It was like a table of pure gold. Intricate drawings carved onto its surface and along its side, like an old story inscribed onto it, before any language put its tale into words. It was beautiful, and its terrible beauty stirred his heart more than if he stared into the eyes of the love of his life. But the lust it excited soured just as quickly, turning into a dark obsession. He had to claim it as his own. He reached out to the water and just as he disturbed the waves, the table sank, taking its mesmerizing beauty and story and secrets with it. Clutching the gold comb, the owner vowed that the golden table would belong to him and him alone.

The next day, over the protests of his workers, the owner drove a dozen high-shouldered oxen to the great rock where the River Mumma stayed. None of his workers accompanied him, refusing even his direct orders. He fixed mighty chains to the oxen and waited for the midday. When the sun shone overhead, the table reappeared. The owner dove into the wa-

ter and hitched the chains to the table before it had a chance to sink. He bobbed at the surface, shouted commands to his oxen team, but before they could move, the chains snapped taut. The owner barely had a chance to glimpse the table before it dragged the chains, and the oxen team attached to them, under the waves.

The owner thrashed about in the water, caught in the undertow of the water's current, the tangle of chains, and the desperately terrified keening oxen. Something lashed against his foot, then dragged him under the waves. Only then did he have a moment to recognize the River Mumma against the darkness of the water. Her teeth green as the barnacles under a rotting boat. Wizened hands, long and veiny. Flexing claws as sharp as shark's teeth. Her red eyes against the shadow of her face, framed by her hair, which floated lifeless, like seaweed caught in the swirling eddies of water.

The river claims all who try to remove that which does not belong to them. And that is why the duppies of all who try haunt the bridges of rivers as the noonday sun passes overhead.

Desmond let a silence settle over them. There was no awkwardness to it, though it wasn't quite the amiable quiet between friends. Lij observed the flames with the intensity of them possibly being extinguished without his constant stare.

A wary itch tickled at the edge of Desmond's mind,

like the ghost of a presence. Something was wrong. A primitive part of his brain, some survival instinct he'd long learned to listen to, urged him to full attention. The stillness grew thick with measure. More an awareness of not being alone than anything else. A fistful of dry brush in his hands, he cocked his head, craning it toward any hint of sound, any careless crackle of leaves or snap of a branch. Nothing. But the nothing chilled him even more. No birdsong. No frog warble. No cicada hum. No smattering of night noise. Only the palpable silence.

"Shhh." Desmond put a lone finger to his lips.

Lij matched the gesture as if Desmond made too much noise with the movement.

Grabbing his tan-handled cane, he twirled it once with a flourish, tipped his hat to Lij, and crept to the edge of their camp. Desmond circled with his back to the child while scanning the forest line. "Lij, stay behind me."

The boy looked up, turned about as if he'd been called upon in class, then shook his head.

"Lij!" Desmond spoke in a stern stage whisper through clenched teeth, but Lij turned his attentions back to the flames.

"I think he knows you're surrounded." A man suddenly appeared, within an arm's reach, as if stepping from Desmond's shadow. Desmond casually took in the man, not betraying any surprise, though he hadn't heard a whisper of his approach. Powerfully built, he wore a blue shirt over dun trousers. A maroon print shawl wrapped about his head, neck, and shoulders. Desmond couldn't place the man's accent. He had none of the affected drawl of a man from of Tejas, but there wasn't any trace of an Albion accent. Yet he spoke English with the same ease as wearing an uncomfortably fitting shoe. He pronounced each word slowly and clearly, precise, the way he moved.

Desmond's face flashed hot again. Clamminess settled along his skin followed by queasiness. A fog clotted his mind. He grew nearly faint with a sudden wooziness. At his peak, he'd cuff the man senseless, but with his spreading sickness, he had his doubts. His hand slowly extended toward his cane.

"I wouldn't do that if I were you. We might get the wrong impression and think that you were being . . . inhospitable." The man's left arm remained down, stiff and deliberate. The man slowly turned it. A glint of metal reflected from it. A pulse cannon had replaced his forearm. The man nodded toward the camp. Figures emerged from the woods, stepping into shafts of moonlight. The shadows of leaves dappled their faces. They each wore similar blue shirts over red leggings, with their own maroon print shawls draped about them. The man held out his good hand. Desmond passed him the cane. The man examined the handle, gave it a slight turn, and, with a flick of his thumb, freed the sword of its scabbard. Returning the blade to its place, he kept hold of the weapon.

"Me and the boy were just out camping." Desmond hoped the sweat that sealed his shirt to him and glossed his forehead would not be interpreted as suspicious. His mind spun, dulled by his muddle-headedness, slowly sinking into a dizzying sleep.

"In sovereign territory? During a border dispute?" The man didn't bother to hide not believing him.

"We figured we were far enough from the conflict." Desmond tugged at his pocket square. He paused to allow the surrounding men to measure his movements, before daubing his head.

"Well, it's about to storm." The man turned to Lij and smiled warmly. "Why don't you come back with us as our guests? We'll find you some proper accommodations."

"Do we have a choice?" Desmond asked.

"We are all free agents. You have nothing but choice." The man squinted. "My friend, you do not look well."

"I'm fine. The boy is my charge. He must be . . ." Desmond's eyes turned upward into his skull. His world blurred and darkened as he collapsed.

IV.

Untold Stories

WITH THE IRREGULAR JOSTLING, through his groggy haze, Desmond pictured himself strung between two men like a deer carcass on a pole. Though vaguely aware that he was being carried on a crude stretcher, Desmond's mind swam, unable to piece together his surroundings. His eyes fluttered open for a few moments. Their leader moved with stealthy economy, no wasted movements, gliding through the woods like the shadow of a bird. By comparison, Lij stomped through the undergrowth. Thumbing at berries, he picked up the occasional stick to beat branches back with, before losing interest and tossing it away. The men turned the makeshift stretcher from the woods onto the main road. When they emerged from the last stand of trees, the high walls of a city rose before them.

Desmond's chest hitched with an anticipatory cough. With their heavy machinery, their spires of smokestacks, the vent of steam through their arteries, most cities vibrated like a distant engine. A pall of engine smoke fouled most large metropolises. The rhythm of the clockwork of the cities sent a thrum through the surrounding countryside. Not so here. The city had a measured breath to it, as if meditating in harmony to its surroundings. Or perhaps the threat of dawning sleep colored his imagination.

The urban sprawl of squat earthen buildings trailed into the woods, layered, unobtrusive, camouflaged by nature, inadvertent interruptions to the greenways. The shapes of the buildings slipped like a groove in the land, adhering to the contours of the landscape. The walls around the city jutted like earthen teeth from a broken jaw. Trees opened up, hiding houses within them. Thick walls enclosed homes, stacked on top of one another like blocks overgrown with grass.

There was a goat.

"Welcome to Wewoka," the leader said.

Eyelids heavy from the numbing darkness, Desmond's head pounded. Pressure throbbed from behind his eyes. The buildings canted at odd angles, both gleaming and covered in green, like metallic, striped trees. Glimmers of daylight seared his eyes. His skin was set aflame by fever, as if flensed from his bones with a hot blade. Figures moved about, nameless and shapeless. Turning toward him. Backing away from him. He closed his eyes again.

Desmond woke to the clank and whir of machinery. A metallic screen loomed in his face. As his eyes focused on it, the smooth countenance of an automaton came into view. Desmond jumped in alarm, his movement cut short by the restraint on his arm. He tugged at the strap before realizing both arms were bound to the bed. An orange light began to flash on top of the automaton's head as it silently whirred out of the room.

Desmond studied the strange architecture of the room. The entryway was a large arch made of brass. Similar brass archways lined the hallway. A glass partition formed the door, and the main window was a long stretch of thick glass. Many rooms, like hidden compartments, lined the cold, twisting hallways. Automatons rolled through the hallways, occasionally stopped by someone who read their recordings and then peered at Desmond as though he were an exhibit at a zoo.

The wall thrummed with activity. A series of bellows within them, passing air though filters, he presumed, scrubbing the air. Plants lined his outside window, a thick mat of greenery along a ledge.

The man who led the group of people who captured him wandered into the room. His bearing suggested a soldier. His skin a deep sepia, almost matching Desmond's. He removed his red turban and hung it on a rack beside the door. Two stripes of hair an inch wide bisected his head: one from temple-to-temple, the other at a right angle from center of forehead to the base of his skull; a small braid at each end. Earrings, small silver clockwork gears, dangled from his lobes. A turquoise necklace draped his throat. A series of silver armbands wrapped around his right bicep. His left arm had changed. The appendage had been swapped out and was much more natural in appearance, though made of brass. A small hand pulse had been mounted to his forearm. His belt was ornamented with silver and gears. He focused his intense eyes on Desmond.

"You're awake," the man said in his accented English.

"Where's the boy?" Desmond answered. He drew against the restraints again as he attempted to sit up. With the number of interrogations he had conducted as a member of the *Niyabingi,* being on this side of the handcuffs felt unnatural.

"What's your name?"

Desmond remained silent.

"He's safe. You'll see him soon enough. Where do you come from?"

Desmond turned away from the man and stared out the large window.

"Not feeling talkative? Just so you know, we are running your fingerprints. The League of Nations has negotiated a shared database of known or wanted figures. It's only a matter of time before we learn who you are and why you're here."

Desmond's eyes flicked to him.

"That caught your attention," the man said.

"I need to see the boy. Make sure he's safe," Desmond said.

"I can arrange that."

"And I need to speak to someone in charge."

"I think you misunderstand the precise nature of your situation. Being shackled to a bed is not exactly a position of strength to begin making demands."

"You misunderstand," Desmond turned toward him. "We may need . . . asylum."

With a weight pressing against his chest, Desmond's eyes snapped open. He hadn't been aware that he had fallen asleep. A pressure straddled him. Someone moved their hands along his body. He made out a dark figure as if glimpsed through a mirror dimly. Desmond struggled to catch his breath.

"I can see you. Alone. In the dark. Under the sheets like a small boy afraid of the monster under the bed," Cayt's voice said.

"Who dem people you take fe fool?" Desmond said.

"Get off me, nuh."

"No matter what you do, no matter where you run, you will lead me to him. Your time is coming. Some things are inevitable."

She bent low, as if to kiss him. She stroked his face. Her hands danced about his throat, slowly tightening about it, choking him.

Desmond sat up in bed.

"What's the matter?" Glancing up from a folder of papers at Desmond's movement, the man guarded the door.

"Duppy a-ride me." The restraints cut so hard into him when he jolted awake, Desmond checked his wrists to make sure he wasn't bleeding.

"Come again? There was no one here. Definitely no . . . duppy?"

"It was nothing. A night terror."

Rolling over to examine his wound as best he could, given the loosened restraints, he saw a small patch of bandage clinging to his side. Desmond leaned back into the bed, feeling every year of his life. He used to daydream about settling down. With five or six children, a small, olive-colored house with white burglar bars along each window and a large yard. His wife would garden; it'd be their shared passion. They'd grow breadfruit, cho cho, guava, gungo peas, and soursop. They'd live a simple life and it would be everything.

The reflections along the glass window made the two men marching down the hallway appear like an entire troop. They took positions on either side of the outer entry arch. A woman walked behind them, holding Lij's hand. She had fine, chiseled features. High cheekbones and with a lighter complexion like tanned hide, she carried herself with a regal air but without any of the officious fussiness he'd come to expect from bureaucrats. Desmond wasn't certain, but he would've sworn she brushed hands with the leader before he took his post at the entrance.

"I'll be right here," he said.

"You've made that pretty obvious." She opened a box of chocolates, popped a ball into her mouth, and tucked the box away into her purse. She wore a full, floor-length skirt gathered at the waist with ruffles at the knee. Trimmed with a ruffle which came only to the shoulders, her long-sleeved blouse had a cape attached which reached her fingertips. Her blouse barely covered her breasts and left a few inches of her midriff exposed. This accentuated the slight bump of her belly. She crossed her arms in front of the gap due to Desmond's lingering gaze.

An automaton whirled into the room, accompanied by an old man.

"Place your arm in the sleeve," a metallic voice commanded from an unseen speaker on the automaton as it released Desmond's arm restraint.

Desmond ignored it.

"Place your arm into the sleeve or you will be designated 'hostile' and we will send someone in to . . . assist you."

Desmond inspected it. The sleeve amounted to a hole in the automaton with a cloth cuff to it. Desmond slipped his arm into the opening. The cuff inflated until it fit snugly around his arm. The cuff pulsed, as if the automaton were trying to suck his arm through a straw. With a hiss, the sleeve deflated and the automaton withdrew from the room.

The old man busied himself in the corner of the room. Gray hairs sprouted from beneath his black turban. A black handkerchief knotted about his neck. An opened black vest covered his long, draping shirt. Crushing roots in a small bowl, he poured water into it and dipped a cloth in the mixture. He approached Desmond but first held out the cloth for his inspection. Desmond didn't flinch, only eyed him as the man daubed him about the neck. The cloth was a welcome cool to the touch. The old man murmured to himself, "hear the owl, respect panther, stare with snake's eye," in a slight chant barely audible to Desmond. The old man turned Desmond's face from one side to the next.

Satisfied with his evaluation, the man left the room.

The woman circled the room. Her cape draped behind her as if held aloft by invisible wires. She made her way to the foot of Desmond's bed, making a show of studying his face. She let go of Lij's hand. The boy glanced up at her and then scrambled up into the bed with Desmond. He grimaced briefly as the boy snuggled into the crook of his arm, kneeing his bandaged area.

"You didn't worry that our medicine man practiced primitive ways on you?" the woman asked at long last. Her English was less strained than her compatriot's.

"In Jamaica, we have those who practice *obayifo*. Obeah. The Science." Noting that no flicker of recognition registered in any of their eyes, Desmond continued. "It's old healing. The obeah men comfort, but don't replace doctors. Or technology. Or medicine."

"No, the medicine would be the course of antibiotics coursing through your system." The woman made a show of pouring two glasses of water and offering one to Desmond.

Desmond shook his head, declining the offer. "He reminds me of home."

"The way I hear it, you're a long way from home." The woman took a long sip of her water, maintaining her level gaze at Desmond. Cocking her head slightly, she reminded him of Lij and his way of staring, which made it seem like she read his soul.

"Sometimes, I think that I don't know what that means anymore." Desmond shut his eyes.

"What's your name?"

"Come, nuh. You have me at a disadvantage."

"You asked for me. A person in charge. Trust has to begin somewhere."

"Desmond Coke. And yours?"

"Now, see, names should be guarded. Your true name has power." She smiled to let him know she meant no harm. "My friend back there goes by Inteus. That is his calling name. In your language, his name translates to Has No Shame."

"Calling name?" Desmond asked.

"The name we call him. You may call me Kajika."

"Perhaps I gave up my name too easily."

"You don't strike me as a man careless about anything, Mr. Coke."

"How long have you been tracking us?"

"We detected your incursion as soon as you crossed our borders. You were monitored the entire time, but then you strayed too near to our maglev lines and became a security risk. We're under constant terrorist alert." Kajika nodded her head. Inteus handed her Desmond's cane. "You have no jurisdiction to carry weapons on sovereign land."

"Where I come from, I have free license to carry such a weapon."

"I had noticed the accent. What did you do that gave you such license?"

"Private security. Me and the boy were long overdue for a vacation." Desmond oddly over-enunciated each word, suddenly self-conscious of his accent. "We thought we would travel as widely as possible."

"Well, we can't just let anyone across our borders."

"Thus we're your prisoners." Desmond raised his shackled hands.

"More like uninvited guests. But guests nonetheless." Kajika motioned to the handcuffs.

Inteus made a face of protest. They exchanged a few words in another language. Kajika crossed her arms and stared at the handcuffs with an air of finality. Though she projected no obvious airs of power, he unfastened the first. She gestured to the second. She turned back to Desmond. "You're not going to be a problem, are you?"

"No, mum," he said. "As your guest, that would be rude."

"Indeed." She hurried Inteus. "Besides, if you did anything rash, you'd prove Inteus right. And he becomes insufferable when he's right."

"But I am still detained for questioning."

"Of course. How have you enjoyed your interrogation

so far?" Kajika possessed a certain charm which both beguiled and disarmed.

Desmond rubbed his wrists; he couldn't help but relax a bit. "I've had worse."

"My apologies. May I ask, what's your son's name?"

"My son?" Desmond let the word roll off his tongue as if truly hearing it for the first time. Lij climbed down from the bed. He moved to the wall and pressed his palm flat against it. As he turned to Desmond, a smile flashed brief as lightning across the night sky. He leaned into the wall, placing his ear against it. The boy closed his eyes, enjoying whatever he heard.

"The boy." Kajika arched a single, knowing eyebrow.

"He's . . . my kin. Not of my blood, but family nonetheless."

"Sounds complicated. I'm sure I'd love to hear the full story of it sometime." The words came out of her without sarcasm or hint of pressing. Simply matter-of-fact. "Does he have a name?"

"You can call him Lij."

"You learn quickly."

"It was the name chosen for him. He has yet to choose his own name. His own way."

"And you wish to give him that chance?" Kajika studied him with the expert eye of a jeweler making an appraisal.

"Something like that." Desmond turned away. "At the very least, we hoped to disappear near the border of the Five Civilized Tribes. Maybe blend in among you."

"Only those who listen to Albion's propaganda know us as the 'Five Civilized Tribes.' We're more of a collective of independent nations. Think of us as regionalisms that govern ourselves, much like the League of Nations. Officially, Albion deals with us as the Assembly of First Nations. Many among us still refer to ourselves as the *Niitsitapi,* the Real People. It is the First Nations which negotiates trade with Albion for our drug technology and limited mineral rights. It is the First Nations which is allied with Canada. You are among the Seminole now. Each of the tribes has our own discrete communities. Hide Me. The Woods Lament For Me. Disturb Me if You Dare."

"Where I come from, we have a long history of taking in those who seek to escape Albion's bondage," Desmond said.

"So it has always been true among the Seminole. We're proud of our heritage. Before Albion landed at Roanoke, before Jamestown, before Plymouth Rock, Lucas Vásquez de Ayllón called his settlement San Miguel de Gualdape. He forced Africans to build the homes, thus launching slavery. Our people moved inland to get away from the invaders.

"Soon, disease and starvation ravaged the colony.

"When Ayllón grew sick and died, the people of the colony divided, taking arms against any who presumed to play leader. So, while their leadership was in disarray, the Africans rebelled and fled to live among our people. We created a mixed settlement. And so it would go. Was this your way of getting around to asking for asylum?"

Desmond sat up as best he could. "Do we even have a case for asylum?"

"That's what I'm here to determine. People run for a variety of reasons. Criminals. Political prisoners. Scandal. To start over. Fear or hope, which is it? So far all I see is a relatively young man . . ."

"Relatively?" Desmond asked with a wry smile.

"I was being polite." She returned his smile. "A man with a young boy out camping on the sovereign border of the First Nations. From the looks of your clothes, you spent some time near Tejas. So, either you enjoy camping in areas hotly contested by Albion, or you seek to hide."

"Perhaps I simply like the sound of armaments at night. I find the shelling rather soothing."

Kajika pursed her lips. "A man with secrets."

"Aren't we all?"

"I've no interest in exhuming a man's secrets, as long as those secrets pose no threat to my people. Do you pose a threat to us?"

"I'm . . . not sure." Trust had to begin somewhere. The Maroon loved their *jijifo,* what they called their "evasive maneuvers," which amounted to lies within agendas meant to confuse outsiders. With Kajika, there was a directness, a certain transparency, which proved no less difficult to navigate. Desmond gestured for a glass of water.

"Intriguing. That's a dangerously honest answer." Kajika slid a glass over to him.

"I wanted to repay your hospitality with the truth. As long as it doesn't endanger us." Desmond took the glass, relieved to have something to do with his hands.

"Fair enough," Kajika said. "Your country knows something about fighting off the Albion forces."

"Cudjoe, Nanny, Accompong, and the other military Maroon leaders fought and expelled the Albion forces from Jamaica nearly two centuries ago. Though we weren't Maroon, my family lived near a city called Nanny Town, which had been completely leveled during an Albion raid. The Maroon left the ruins standing as a solemn reminder of our fate should we ever lower our guard. People say that the duppies of those who died in the battle still haunted the ruins."

"Duppies?" She arched an eyebrow.

"You'd call them ghosts. Spirits."

"We all live with the ghosts of our past. And we have had our own 'Nannys.' The Seminoles learned much from our experience in Florida. Slaves often escaped one or two at a time. With its thick bush and dangerous reptiles, the land protected them. Seminoles became used to admitting those who were different. With us as their home base, the ex-slaves would sneak into Georgia or Alabama to fetch their families."

"I can't imagine that Albion turned a blind eye to this." Desmond adjusted himself into a new position as Lij climbed back onto the bed with him.

"Albion feared friendship between the African and native peoples. The Giant to the North would never accept an independent, armed, free black community. The very idea of our friendship, a safe haven, threatened to destroy their slaveholding ways. Nor did they want native communities on their borders who harbored blacks. They feared sabotage, revolt, subversion, or any form of haven for runaways. So they tried to drive wedge between the peoples. They went so far as to promote slavery among the native peoples. When that didn't work as well as they expected, Albion 'Patriots' amassed forces in order to prepare to annex Florida. Business interests and government officials made plans to carve up Florida like it was a dessert. They deployed troops prepared to burn down villages."

"The 'Giant to the North' would never let you be." The story had a familiar ring to Desmond. To this day, Albion harassed Jamaican sovereign territory with air incursions.

"It's like a young child who wants everything it sees for its own," Desmond said. "They kept citizens and Parliament in the dark for their own good. Created a situation so fraught that the Seminoles saw no choice but to attack the Giant to the North first. That began the series of conflicts. Regent Van Buren passed their 'Indian Removal Act.' They fixed it in their minds to herd us. They wanted to move us to the Oklahoma and Arkansas territories. We knew it would only be a matter of time before they would want to settle there too. Wildcat and John Horse thought about going to Mexico, but Lalawethika of the Shawnee, brother of Tecumseh, had a different vision. He preached that Albion came from the sea, Spawn of the Great Serpent. Children of the Evil Spirit. He knew that Albion dreamt boldly, but their Western Design would take time."

Kajika paused, considering the best way to continue.

"Lalawethika, too, had a plan: leading the Tecumseh Confederacy and forming a large multi-tribal community. He wanted us to withdraw, not to Oklahoma or Arkansas on Albion's terms, but travel further west and north. It gave us time to fortify, be away from their diseases. Though it took a while to convince the Plains Nations, the Shawnees and Delawares, eventually the tribes moved. As far as Albion was concerned, one day we were blocking their migration across the land, the next day we were gone. We established the First Nations territory. Albion's expansion crept slowly westward, with all due caution as they were afraid that they would encounter us and be harried along the way. By the time they reached our border, we were entrenched and fortified. They decided that it was wiser to grant us independence and sovereignty than war.

"The Seminoles, those whom Albion calls 'Black Indians,' were more immune to the diseases brought in by those of Albion, so we tend to live on the borders of the First Nations as a buffer zone. Sometimes, we serve as ambassadors."

"Is that what you are? An ambassador?"

"It's as good a word as any. We were always seen as experts on Albion, on their brand of diplomacy, their armaments, and their motives. We understand their strengths and weaknesses, their language and defenses." Kajika was cautious and smart. Not revealing the extent of her diplomatic business with him and leaving no clear understanding of the extent of her power or duties.

"But the wolf is at your door again."

"Indeed," Kajika replied. "Destiny is upon us and the wolf is as voracious as ever for resources to plunder. Makes me question any who wish to come here."

"For they might be the eyes of the wolf."

"They might. The wolf does so love its innocent disguises." Kajika cast a long, unwavering glance toward Lij.

The boy pretended not to see her.

Kajika turned back to Desmond. "So I ask again, are you officially asking for asylum?"

"I . . . don't know. We haven't made up our minds whether we want to stay or simply have safe passage until we reach Canada."

"Let me know when you make up your mind. A formal request would put me in quite a bind during these delicate times. And I hate making too many decisions of state before breakfast."

For the first few days, Inteus stationed two guards at the door of Desmond's *chickee,* a small house with thick earthen walls and a grass-thatched roof. Lij enjoyed the open layout because it gave him room to run. From the porch, Desmond observed the people who walked by. Acclimatizing to its customs and particular brand of bustle, he'd gotten a sense of Wewoka. Without the lens of a fever-induced vision, it proved to be a dense, vertical city of narrow, terraced streets with expansive walkways. Largely devoid of motor traffic, any point could be reached by foot in fifteen minutes. Pictures painted on the sidewalks provided a colorful trail. With a central street lined with shops bustling with commerce, the noise and smell were different from what he was used to. Wewoka had none of the overworked smokestacks from innumerable factories; much of the city was made up by parks. The air had a hint of ozone to it.

A collection of buildings sprouted at the heart of the city. Gleaming green and metallic spires in the distance, the sun reflected from their solar panels. A mushroom-like structure drew in sewer water from its "roots" and funneled it to its dome. Solar energy evaporated the water, which was then collected and released throughout the streets, watering the surrounding green spaces. Photovoltaic panels lined solar drop towers. Titanium dioxide reacted with ultraviolet rays and smog, filtering and dissipating them. They had developed similar technology in Jamaica. Vertical gardens and vegetation covered the steep towers of housing units and work offices. The exterior vertical gardens filtered the rain, which was reused with liquid wastes for farming needs. A deep calm reverberated through the city, quiet preserved like a commodity.

Desmond wanted to investigate Wewoka more, visit its shops, dine at its eateries, explore its trains, but Inteus forbade him. While Kajika pondered their case, he was on virtual house arrest. So, each morning, he rose and climbed to the roof of his *chickee* under the early morning rays to perform the forms. The gentle martial movements didn't tug at his stitches as much as he feared.

A mechanical eagle circled in ever-widening loops before disappearing behind a wall of low-lying clouds.

"What do you call those?" Inteus asked, indicating Desmond's actions.

"You have a disturbing habit of sneaking up on me." Desmond continued with his movements.

"A strange name for them." Inteus kept out of reach.

"We call them the forms. The Maroon teach bangaran from one generation to the next. When I was being taught, my instructor told me to think of them this way: just as we tell our stories over and over to preserve and pass them along, the forms are like a dance meant to reinforce and transmit the techniques. I remember the first time I saw someone full-on in a fight. I thought to myself, 'Me neva wan fe romp with dem boy deh, suh! Jus like dat, dem break wan man foot.'" Desmond smiled at the memory.

Inteus studied him for a few minutes with a scrupulous eye on his technique. "Kajika is ready to see you."

"You two seem . . . close." Desmond wound down his routine.

"Only fitting, with her being my wife."

"I can imagine such an arrangement complicates matters of state."

"She has her duty; I have mine. At home, our duty is to one another. It's not so different, I imagine, between you and the boy." Inteus nodded toward the *chickee*.

Lij watched from the entryway.

"As I said, duties of the heart sometimes complicate duties to the state."

Inteus led Desmond and Lij's escort group through the streets of Wewoka. Women strode along the cobbled sidewalks in their patchwork skirts displaying bands of alternating colors. Strings of beads wrapped around and around their necks until they were completely covered. Men wore *foksikpayahkis,* simple-cut, smock-like shirts which went down to their knees, black applique work sewn onto their front plackets. Some wore vests or felt hats rather than turbans, a bit of appropriation of Albion fashion.

The group passed a maze of buildings arranged like stacked puzzle boxes, until they reached a low-slung building with heavy wooden doors. Inteus escorted Desmond and Lij to a large office. Gaslit fixtures lined the wall, incongruous to the décor of the room. A glass-fronted grandfather clock contained a rotating cylinder winding gears, almost like a concession meant to make

Albion visitors feel more comfortable. Bookshelves and a desk with two chairs in front of it dominated the room. The shelves lined one wall of the room from ceiling to floor, filled with books and artifacts. Biographies and histories nearly monopolized the topics, though books on religion and philosophy occupied their fair share of shelf space.

"Do you like books?" Kajika asked.

Lij all but froze. Only the slightest movement of his head in her direction acknowledged her at all.

"As you can see, I like books a lot." She gestured toward the shelves.

"I like to read," Lij said.

"A boy your age who loves to read. What kind of books do you like?"

"All kinds. James Baldwin. Toni Morrison. James Joyce. Shakespeare."

"Those"—Kajika glanced toward Desmond—"are awfully adult books."

"I'm sorry."

"There's no need to apologize. It's just . . ."

Lij turned away. He no longer met her eyes, no matter how she attempted to put herself in his line of vision. Lij busied himself with a cornhusk doll and a stone carving of a buffalo taken from one of the shelves. He tapped the buffalo then held it to his ear to listen.

One of his men moved to take Lij to a different room. Desmond tensed. Inteus waved the man off and gestured for them to leave. Then he took a position near the door.

Kajika padded back to her desk, circling it with extra accommodation given to her belly. Neat and orderly, with the only personal object on it a framed photograph of a much younger Kajika and Inteus. Relieved to be off her feet, she sighed as she sank into her chair.

"Who are you, Mr. Desmond Coke?" Kajika opened one of her desk drawers. She popped a chocolate ball in her mouth, but didn't offer one, and slid the drawer shut.

"I'd guess you already have an answer."

"By now you're quite acquainted with Inteus, our chief of security."

"Your husband."

"Indeed. Well, he's quite good at what he does. Resourceful, too. I've learned not to ask too many questions about how he gathers his information. Especially so quickly. He spins quite a tale about you."

"I'm not at all that interesting," Desmond said.

"Perhaps it's just rumor, then. He's heard that a member of a Jamaican dissident group, the Order of the *Niyabingi*, became an aide to a prominent family. Later reports indicate that he disappeared with a young boy. The boy was considered of great importance to Jamaica's ruling class. Many interests, both within and without Jamaica, pursue them to this day."

"It's complicated. In Jamaica we have a saying: 'Trust no shadow after dark.' These days, our world is full of shadows."

"Again I ask, who are you, Desmond Coke? More shadows we don't need."

"I am Jamaican by birth, Rastafarian by faith, and *Niyabingi* by mission. We organized to fight imperialism wherever we found it. Even if it meant our own mad leaders. Some consider the *Niyabingi* terrorists, though the irony is that most of the *Niyabingi* consider me a traitor for abandoning my mission."

"For the boy?"

"As you say. And many intend to capture us, him, for their own purposes. Borders mean nothing to some people."

"You are a far-blown leaf from a forest a good way away. Though long removed from your roots, you are still part of the tree."

"I feel like I've been on the run ever since I left Garlands. From the time of my father's death, the *Niyabingi* claimed and trained me for their secret missions. I still live for the mission; it just now includes a young boy in tow."

"One thing I've surmised is that whoever is after you won't forget you."

"With the life I chose, wherever you lie your head, you go to sleep with the fear of waking up with a knife to your throat. I don't want that life for Lij. It's like dying. Every day. I'd hoped that in Albion, things would be different."

"Albion loves the breadth of its shadow too much. Their people love or at least indulge the rule of their kings," Kajika said.

"Or queens," Desmond said.

Kajika smiled at this. "Or regents. Or senators. No matter how benevolent the ruler, the military drives the empire. Armaments feed the beast. And soldiers who train for war need a war for purpose."

"It's all the same. Be it the Obeahists wresting for the control of the spirit of our people. Or the Kabbalists working out the Tree of Life and the mysteries of the Divine Throne, all of which amounts to a cabal of Albion's business interests draped in mystical nonsense. Or simply governments with their rulers. And soldiers."

"Our warriors are for defense," Kajika said.

"A beast is a beast," Desmond insisted.

"Not so. Some beasts have their teeth pulled. They prosper by building and innovating rather than destroying and conquering. And warriors can choose to live by a code of peace."

"A beast by any other name . . ." Desmond wondered if

he pushed her too much. Debating the philosophy of rules and empires indulged time he didn't have to spare. He grew frustrated, not seeing the point of all of this talk. He couldn't help feeling as if he were failing a test he didn't understand the rules of. Almost as if she tried to paint a picture for him or, rather, figure out a picture of him.

Kajika pushed away from her desk and got up. She paced back and forth a few steps. "Let me try it this way. It's about priority. Soldiers are necessary when faced with an enemy who wishes to bully or overrun their neighbor. Sometimes violence, as a last resort, is the only language a mad dog understands. Is it so different in Jamaica?"

"We let others keep their dictators, kings, and political games. We content ourselves with ambitious fools who love gamesmanship and arguments, vying for power and respect. As long as our people prosper and are safe and . . ."

". . . the trains run on time?" Kajika arched one of her eyebrows in that annoying way of making him feel like he'd walked into a rhetorical trap.

"Something like that. We're content in our isolation to argue amongst ourselves."

"And when the argument comes to your door?"

"Then a beast is a beast is a beast," Desmond conceded.

"See? We're more alike than you may think."

"Excuse me, Kajika, but I don't see where any of this is getting us."

"I just want you to see what you're stepping into before you commit. And I want a better understanding of what we're getting. We're proud of our history, even the blemishes. The Assembly of First Nations won the Three-Day War, which Albion dubbed a breakdown of diplomacy—'a tragic misunderstanding'—where they had their asses handed to them, in other words. Yet here they were, on the verge of another one."

"The border skirmishes?"

"Skirmishes? Thwarted incursions is more like it. With one hand they try to negotiate very publicly for limited mineral rights. All the while, they spy on us, violate our borders, and continue to test us."

"The trade negotiations are pretext?"

"Perhaps. Which is why we have heightened security. You come at either the worst or most convenient of times. I need to understand any threat you bring to my people. You could be the diplomatic equivalent of a flaming bag of shit left on our porch. Hear me now: I don't want to stomp out shit. Not in these shoes."

Kajika smiled again. Her jokes were meant to ease the tension in the air between them, but Desmond knew the face of a lioness ready to tear the meat from his bones to protect her people.

"It's Lij they want. For you, nature is technology. So it is with Lij. He was grown from the cells of one of our great leaders. If names have power, as you say, let me tell you his name: Lij Tafari Makonnen Woldemikael. He ruled his kingdom as the King of Abyssinia, His Imperial Majesty Haile Selassie I. Those of my faith believe he was meant to come back after his death."

"If I understand what you're saying, you may have possibly adopted the messiah of your faith and are raising him?"

"I . . ." Desmond hesitated. "I try not to think about that. All I see is a little boy who I'm protecting from the people who want him. Who would take him, drain his blood, turn his body inside out, and tease his brain apart. Break him down in parts to divine how he was created. 'Reverse engineer the process,' they said. All to figure out what? That he was human?"

"Or more than human," Kajika said.

"He's just a boy."

"So you say. I've seen many things. Heard even more. Inteus informs me that some in Albion hope to develop the mind to be able to read or transmit thoughts. Move objects. Kill with mere concentration."

"Lij would never do that."

"People fear the unknown. People fear the future. People fear an . . . abomination."

"Is that how you see him?" Desmond's voice rose in pitch. He didn't realize how heated the discussion had gotten or how defensive he had become at the idea of anyone threatening Lij. Inteus took two steps closer to him, the movement alone meant to remind Desmond of his presence and situation.

Kajika held up her hand to halt her chief of security. She turned her head at an angle to further study Lij. He trotted the buffalo along the bookshelves, using it to tap along the ledges, whatever rhythm known only to him. "No. He's just a boy. But what life can he have with so many eager to pry him open for his secrets?"

"A life of freedom," Desmond whispered. "That's all any of us seek."

"Not all of us get it."

"So, you'd deny him?"

Kajika walked over to Lij. The cornhusk doll now riding the stone buffalo, he paused his game at her approach. He didn't turn to her but froze like an antelope that had been spotted by a hyena.

"So, this is our security threat?" Kajika said.

"I wouldn't get so close," Inteus said.

"Nonsense."

"I really must insist."

"If you insist any more, I'm going to name your son 'Shits Like Deer.'"

Lij laughed.

She sized him up with a hard stare. Abruptly, her features softened. "My apologies, little one. That was inappropriate."

"*Raasclaat,*" Lij said.

"*Raasclaat.* I'm afraid I don't know this word."

"It's a Jamaican swear word," Desmond said. "It means . . . um, nothing fit for mixed company."

"Now that sounds like some *raasclaat,*" Kajika said. "He has such an odd manner for a boy his age."

"With all due respect, he can hear you." The tone had more teeth to it than he intended. "I suspect that it may be an unanticipated side effect of his [illegible] conception. But he's still a boy. He likes stories."

"Well, he's in luck. We of the First Nations are some of the best storytellers on the planet." She folded herself down, an awkward tangle of arms and legs. Inteus approached to offer a hand, but she waved him off. While she tried to find a comfortable position, Kajika scooted down close to Lij. The boy said nothing but didn't move away, either. She glanced at Desmond, who nodded to her. She cleared her throat.

Some stories were only told when words failed. When whatever truth scrabbled about in the dark, in secret places that defined a people, bubbled to the surface and found its voice spoken in a language only known to the wind.

Tree at the Center leveled a cool eye at the piece of mica before him. He burnished its edges with the meticulous care of a father swaddling his child for the first time. When he first sat at his spinning wheel, he could not see the shape in the mica that he would bring out. He feared the voice who sang the music of his inspiration was gone forever. Only in the last few days had he begun to hear a new voice to carry him through.

"What are you doing, Father?" He Interrupts asked.

"What does it look like?"

"An eagle's claw." He Interrupts inspected the sculpture. "But I thought that all business was set aside for today."

"This isn't business. It's personal." Tree at the Center's mouth curled weakly into a smile as if testing to see if he still could form one. He tousled the young boy's hair.

"Is it for Mother?"

"It is. Many people wish to honor Whispers on the Breeze. When a family member dies, the entire village mourns."

He Interrupts knitted his brow, deep in thought. "What can I give her?"

"We have our origins in stories, in words spoke into creation. You must give her part of your story."

"But I have no story to give."

"That's not true. You two had a shared story. That's what you leave her."

"What was your story?" He Interrupts pointed to the eagle claw.

Tree at the Center glanced from the boy to the artifact, then back to the boy. He set his teeth as if chewing on an idea. Finally, he cleared his throat to speak.

"One day a long time ago, a woman had wandered far from the Road Much Traveled and gotten lost in the woods. Hungry and faint, she collapsed on the bank of a great river. It was cold and rainy, as both the sun and the moon hid themselves in the sky.

"The Father of Eagles spied her. Keen of eye, wings the span of a village, the proud bird circled her. It took pity on the sight of the young woman dying. The Father of Eagles swooped down, the beating of its mighty wings bent young trees, yet the woman did not stir. It lifted her up gently and searched for a village.

"The great bird warmed her body and brought her food. Its heart grew to love her. So it told her stories. The Father of Eagles told her of the secret songs of the birds. It told her of their dances. It told her of the laws of birds. All these things and more it shared with her.

"Then one day, she nestled under its wing while it flew. The earth slept under snow and the wind moaned through bare branches. In the distance, smoke rose. The Father of Eagles flew towards the smoke and found a village of the People before our people, their names long forgotten. It landed on the village's edge.

"'You must go with them, for they are your kind,' the

Father of Eagles said.

"'But I don't want to. I am a stranger to them,' she said.

"'They know the true name of things. They walk with their spirits open. And they will grow to love you as I have. And you shall tell them our stories.'

"'Will you ever return?' she asked.

"'One day I shall come back and carry away the entire village on my back.'

"And so our stories have come down through our mothers, one generation after the next. Passing on our heritage and knowledge to our children."

He Interrupts shuffled from one foot to the next in thoughtful silence. He studied his empty hands for a moment and then spoke again with a seriousness to his voice much older than his few years. "I'm still not sure that I have a story to offer her."

"Much can be learned from listening to those with much experience. Maybe it's time for you to show me the craft you have learned. See how well I have prepared you in our way of life." Tree at the Center scattered a few blocks of chert around them. "Choose your own. The one that speaks to you."

He Interrupts cocked his head as if wanting to ask a question but thinking better of it. He rolled a couple of the blocks about, inspecting each of them. If one particularly intrigued him, he picked it up and tapped it with a stone. Narrowing down his choices to the final two, he chose the one with the higher pitch to its song. Fine-grained, durable, and carvable, the large stone had no fissures in it, nor any bubbles or other minerals.

"You chose well. Now gather your tools." Tree at the Center stepped away from his table.

He Interrupts approached the table with solemnity, looking over each instrument with great care before picking any of them up. He gripped the antler tine in his hand, weighing its heft. Then he found a hammer-stone which fit snugly into his hand. He sat cross-legged, imitating the posture of his father at work. He held the hammer-stone just above his chosen piece of chert and waited. Tree at the Center nodded.

He Interrupts struck the stone, tentative at first, judging the flaking of the stone. Soon, the stone began to slowly take the form of a blade. He scraped it to further guide its shape. Tree at the Center nodded with approval, only occasionally making a dissatisfied gurgle, which made He Interrupts shift the angle of his flaking. When the boy was finished, Tree at the Center took the bladelet and hafted it to a handle.

"Am I a man yet?" He Interrupts asked, admiring his handiwork.

"Not yet. I'll let you know." Tree at the Center smiled. "Come, let's walk the Road Much Traveled while you remember the blade's story."

"Remember?"

"We do not create out of nothing but rather from what has

been here before us. You work from a half-remembered idea, and soon the rest of the story will come to you."

The Road Much Traveled passed through the heart of their hamlet, dividing it evenly in two. The pair trekked by a series of wattle-and-daub walled rectangular homes with thatched-roofs. The road wound along the crops of their people: corn, squash, goosefoot, and maygrass. The Road Much Traveled connected all of the villages like a long, winding serpent stretched across the lands.

He Interrupts made an inarticulate noise, drawing Tree at the Center's attention. The boy ground his jaw, caught his father's expectant gaze, then began to speak.

"It is said that the moon connects all life, her beams like threads touching all things like a spider's web. At times, she cannot stand to see what her children do to one another, so she hides her face from them.

"There once was a young boy, one of the People of the Hill, whose mother and father had died. His father's brother took him in, but his uncle was not kind. He worked the boy long and hard, yet fed him seldom and little. He was quick to anger and slow to forgive.

"Now, it was the custom for the older men to walk ahead of the rest when a group went off to trade. The boy was relieved, for it meant that he was away from his uncle at least during the day. That night, however, his uncle fell into a horrifying anger. He stormed into the woods and the

boy followed, fearing for his uncle. His uncle got into a terrible argument with the moon. His shouts echoed for miles. Finally, he drew his knife, for he sought to end the moon's unyielding observation of his life. He slashed wildly at the beams, unable to still the moon's light.

"Finally, the knife slipped from his hand. Fearing that his uncle might injure himself or one of his kinsmen, the boy ran to the fallen blade and threw it into the nearby creek. The uncle dropped to his knees at the water's edge, clutching after the knife. But each time he outstretched his hand, the moon kept it out of reach."

He Interrupts closed his mouth as if satisfied and continued walking along the road.

"Wait one moment," Tree at the Center said. "What happened with the boy? Or his uncle?"

"No story ever ends, but sometimes the telling of it has to. I'm content to know that she is always there, watching over her children. That is what I have to share."

Veering from the Road Much Traveled, He Interrupts followed Tree at the Center deep into the valley. A quiet settled over them, a curtain of reverent silence, which left them somewhat unsettled. Surrounded by thick groves of trees, they followed the creek. The trees seemed to crowd them, to block them at every turn, unspeaking sentries not wanting to share their secrets. Then the forest opened up. From their vantage point, they could take in the entire earthworks.

A large square of platted ground was attended by a smaller one conjoined with a massive circle. Within the vast circle were a series of connected earthen mounds. A wall, nearly two men high, bordered the carefully measured earth. Just beyond the northern wall were several pits of excavated earth.

"We build together. One people coming together in shared purpose," Tree at the Center said as if answering an unasked question. "No matter where we go or how we spread out."

Tree at the Center led He Interrupts to an unfinished mound. He set his mica eagle claw within it. His heart ached, still missing the familiar voice who spoke beauty into his world. He closed his eyes, his lips moving though without sound. When he opened his eyes, he stepped aside to make room for He Interrupts.

"A prayer?" He Interrupts asked.

"There are stories we share and stories we keep to ourselves," Tree at the Center said.

He Interrupts nodded. "Whispers on the Breeze." His set his bladelet alongside the eagle claw and closed his eyes. "Some things can tell when their name is spoken," he said as if answering his father's unasked question.

Tree at the Center stepped back from the mound. "One day, all that will be left of us is our stories. When our tribe has become little more than a faded dream with only our tales left to shape our children and our children's children. But a story only needs a teller for it to be remembered. At night, when the road is free of travelers and the villages are silent, the dream of us will fill the land. There is no death, only movement between worlds.

"Our stories live on after us."

The last words hung in the air like the last notes of a concerto with the audience pausing, too nervous to applaud. Lij said nothing. He glanced at Kajika from the side of his eye, then went back to playing with the cornhusk doll astride her buffalo. Before Desmond could warn her against it, Kajika reached out to pat him on the back. Lij didn't so much as flinch.

There was a knock at her door. A young man entered the chamber and handed Inteus a note. In turn, he went over and whispered in Kajika's ear before handing her the note. She read it and reread it as she returned to Desmond's side.

"It appears that we have captured another guest."

V.

Here Comes the Hotstepper

DESMOND FOLLOWED Kajika and Inteus down a series of stone steps deep beneath the building. Two guards came to attention at their approach. They passed through a set of double doors, then proceeded down a long, winding hallway. Kajika moved with a different air. Her lightness of spirit and casual veneer had been replaced by a hardness. She moved with a determination that dared anyone to bar her way. Inteus marched in step with her, neither behind nor ahead. As he walked, he checked the pulse weapon attached to his arm.

While Desmond wanted to leave Lij with one of the attendants, the boy would have none of it. He clung to Desmond's leg fastidiously. In the name of saving time, Kajika simply allowed him to come, and Desmond suspected that she wanted to keep the pair of them in her sight. Her invitation for him to join her and Inteus fell far short of a request.

They arrived at a large bay window. In the room, a

woman sat in a chair, her arms shackled behind her. Wrapped in layer after layer of clothes, Cayt seemed much smaller. Draped in an ankle-length rifle frock coat, her double-breasted gold leaf vest folded over an open-collared black bib shirt. The gold chain of a pocket watch hooked to a button on her vest and disappeared in the right vest pocket. An empty black tooled-leather buscadero holster was strapped to the left leg of her canvas-colored divided leather skirt. Her black gambler hat and matching fringed gloves were piled neatly in her lap.

"She had these on her." Inteus handed Kajika a hand pulse modified from a Colt Mustang along with three charge cartridges and what appeared to be a man's billfold. Inside was an identification card from the Pinkerton National Detective Agency for a Cayt Siringo.

"The Pinkertons? A bit outside of their jurisdiction, aren't they?" Kajika asked.

"They are a private security guard and detective agency. They have their fingers in a lot of military and corporate intelligence pies. They provide security services to the Albion government on a contractual basis. The ID checks out. We're running a full background check."

They spoke in English. Most times when the two spoke and needed privacy, they shifted to their native tongue. Creek or Miccosukee, Kajika once explained. She spoke five languages and could read a couple more.

So, Desmond knew that they wanted him to hear what was going on.

"She's not speaking. Do you know each other?" Kajika asked. "Don't worry; she can neither see nor hear us through the glass."

"'Know' is a strong word," Desmond said.

Cayt chuckled, her head lowered, her blond hair obscuring her face.

Inteus hit a button on the wall. His voice carried into the room. "Is something funny?"

"I introduced myself to him in Tejas but missed."

At the sound of her voice, Desmond tensed. He flattened his palm against the glass to steady himself.

"You two sound like you have history, Desmond," Kajika said.

"She was the one who shot me. Before that day, I'd never set eyes on her."

"There's something else." Kajika stared at him with those knowing eyes of hers.

Desmond leaned closer to the glass. "It's . . . This may sound strange, but I know her voice. In my dreams. In my mind."

"Borders mean nothing to them; why should walls?" Kajika opened the door and went in, followed by Inteus. "You were caught in violation of First Nations sovereign land."

"I heard tell that you all were accepting all types of folks these days." Cayt met her eyes. Her face a series of hard angles, her skin taut, baked by constant sun. Her eyes dark, with the allure of secrets.

"We like to make new friends," Kajika said.

"Well, I'm the friendly sort." Cayt winked at the window for Desmond's benefit.

"I like your outfit. But no necktie?"

Cayt turned her head like she was trying to brush the hair out of her eyes. "I'm uncomfortable with the idea of anything being tied around my neck. I like your dress. Very Albion fashion-forward."

Kajika bowed slightly. Her emerald green skirt, which matched her blouse and half-cape, had a bustle that almost looked like a bow. "Thank you. I hail from the No-Ass-At-All tribe, so I trust Albion fashion to compensate."

"You're funny, too."

"There are limits to my sense of humor." Despite her joke, Kajika wore no smile and there was no play in her voice.

"Why are you here?" Inteus stepped forward.

"My, aren't you a big one. You the bad cop?" Cayt asked. "I suppose not. The Pinkertons have no official reach here, so you probably don't employ the City Ordained variety, either."

"I'm not in the habit of repeating myself."

"I'm here on behalf of my employer. He wished to negotiate a . . . private trade agreement."

"The Assembly of First Nations is already in negotiations with Albion for trade of gold and natural gas rights," Kajika said.

"That's Albion. My employer would be a private concern."

"And you thought the best way to open negotiations was to begin with some clandestine infiltration?"

"I'm the kind of gal who likes to learn the lay of the land before sitting down for supper."

"Well, now that you have a place at the table, what is it you want?" Kajika asked.

"Well, it's a mite unfriendly to chat with these handcuffs on."

"Just the same, we'll leave those in place." Kajika circled the room, maintaining a wary distance from Cayt.

"Not exactly neighborly, though I understand. Where I'm from, we don't take too kindly to strangers either."

"It's like that Albion saying: 'He's a stranger; hit him on the head!'"

"Something like that," Cayt said.

"And where are you from?"

"That's like asking a gal her age. Not very polite."

"The Matagorda State, in southwestern Tejas," Inteus

said, reading from a report. "Then moved to Chicago as a political consultant before joining the Pinkerton Agency and earning the nickname 'Two-Gun Cayt.'"

"Girl's gotta eat." Cayt relaxed in the chair despite her restraints. She kept her hands still, not even attempting to negotiate the cuffs.

"So, what does your employer want?" Kajika asked.

"First thing, he'd be interested in going into business with you. Perhaps patent some of your technology. He knows the age of steam has nearly run its course and he's looking to the future."

"So he proposes what? A partnership?"

"Assuming you don't want to sell the patents outright."

"Our culture is not for sale. And you don't patent nature."

"You and your techno-shamans just run around giving everything away for free?"

"Techno-shamans? Seriously? Where do you people get your intel? Pulp novels?" Kajika rolled her eyes. There was a slight exasperation before she spoke again, slowly, as if repeating an explanation to a child. "We call them engineers. It's from the Navajo meaning . . . engineers."

For a brief moment, Cayt's sardonic expression cracked for a brief moment, revealing a no-nonsense coldness that could easily sight someone through a telescopic lens and squeeze the trigger. She recovered quickly and put a thin smile on her face. "Consider our offer. The alternative is to go to trial as we sue you for patent infringement."

"The case would be tossed out of whatever court would presume to have jurisdiction."

"Not before it cost you millions. And tied up resources that could go towards more research."

"So, your 'proposal' is for us to trade with you with the 'incentive' of the alternative being pushed into a technology war with you?"

"Again, when you put it that way, it comes off rather rude."

"What's the other thing he wants?" Kajika asked.

"I think you know."

"The boy."

"The boy." Cayt focused on Lij like a tailor taking measurements. "Actually, the pair of them. The boy for my employer, but there's another interested party who put quite the bounty on the other one's head. Dead or alive, as it were."

"Why him?" Kajika glanced over her shoulder toward Desmond.

"Some consider him an outlaw."

"An outlaw to some." Desmond pounded at the intercom button. "Sometimes, that's the only fair response to a reprehensible system. When the powerless seek their own sense of control, 'crime' is what an unjust system produces."

"That one can get quite riled up, can't he?" Cayt turned from him, her thin smile still in place. "Anyways, you have my offer. You hand them over, we can forget this little interruption to my mission."

"I am not some obstacle in your mission," Kajika snapped. "I am not some inconvenient chapter as you pursue your Western Design. I have a story. We have a story and our story demands respect."

"Okay, okay, I get it. You can get riled up too." Cayt stared at the observation window, focusing on Lij. "Why don't y'all go ahead and powwow or whatever it is you do. I'll just wait here."

Inteus closed the door behind him and Kajika. The two of them seemed to huddle about Desmond in silence. The weight of Cayt's words demanded a response, but Desmond didn't want to have the conversation in front of the boy.

"Lij, are you hungry?" Desmond asked. "Why don't you go with Inteus's friend and get something to eat? He'll bring you right back."

Lij pressed a hand against the observation window, studying Cayt as if locked in silent conversation with her. When Desmond touched his shoulder to direct him to

Inteus's assistant, Lij flapped his hands. With a harder nudge from Desmond, Lij shouted, an inchoate, protesting whine. Desmond kept his arm pressed to Lij to keep the boy from clinging to him.

"Lij, could you do me a favor?" Kajika knelt down until she was eye level with him. She pointed to the figurines. "Could you take care of my doll and buffalo? They need to go with Inteus's friend, but they do get lonely when you're not around."

Lij stared at her with his pale green eyes, greeted only by her broad smile. Somewhat mollified, Lij turned to follow Inteus's aide but did not take his hand.

"You're good with him," Desmond said.

"I figure I need the practice." Kajika patted her belly. "If I screw up talking to Lij, well, I can always send him off with you."

Desmond drew the door shut. "What do you think?"

"Worried that we might hand you over?" Kajika asked. "It would certainly be an expedient solution, as none of this is a concern of the First Nations."

"I don't think it was an accident, her being here," Inteus said.

"I'm not a big believer in coincidence," Kajika said.

"I definitely have the feeling that our meeting was arranged by some unseen hand," Desmond said. "The hand of a practiced manipulator."

"To exploit both of us," she said.

"Before she gave me this parting gift"—Desmond patted his side—"I had been approached by someone who represented the interests of Garrison Hearst. He seemed to insinuate that she worked for his competition, Leighton Melbourne."

"Desmond, you sure know how to pique the wrong people's interests," Kajika said.

"And, no offense to Inteus," Desmond continued, "but she's too good to be so conveniently captured."

"If she allowed herself to be captured, then why?"

"Like a laser on a scope. To better sight her target," Inteus said. "Is that what you're thinking?"

"Leaving bread crumbs along her trail, maybe, one way or another, guiding the enemy to your doorstep," Desmond said.

"So, you don't think her offer was genuine?" Kajika's voice dripped with sarcasm.

"The intent was true," Inteus said. "Her employer wants to lay hands on our resources. Industrial espionage with the subtlety of a hammer to the skull."

"They only know one way: violence," Kajika said. "Beneath the power of empire is the problem of justice. Peel that back and beneath the power of justice is the problem of violence."

"Maybe she already told us why she was here,"

Desmond faced the window and thought of Cayt sitting in her detention cell, patient as a spider.

"What do you mean?"

"To 'get a lay of the land.' See your fortifications. Your security measures."

"Yes, but for any of that to be of any use, she'd have to transmit that intelligence to someone," Inteus said.

"Or escape." Desmond met their eyes with alarm.

They moved as a unit, following the hallways back to the detention area. As they rounded the corner, the open door told them what they'd find in the room. A guard lay unconscious at the threshold. The room was empty.

"Lij," Desmond whispered.

He ran first to the commissary and then to Kajika's office. When he opened the door, he found Inteus's aide unconscious.

And the cornhusk doll crushed on the floor.

VI.

Chant Down Babylon

CAYT DUCKED BETWEEN TWO BUILDINGS. The way they were stacked created an alcove and a pool of shadow. She re-gripped her gun but held it low as she peeked around the corner. With the hour late, only a few people meandered along the sidewalk. Her other hand fastened around Lij's hand. Her grasp firm but not painful; it didn't need to be. It only took him witnessing her beating the aide senseless to settle the boy down. Any time a whimper began to build in his chest, she tightened her hand.

"It's not much further." Cayt pressed her back against the wall. Her breath came in deep, controlled gasps. "If you can keep quiet a little while longer, everything will be okay. If you make a fuss, I'll do to these kind folks what I did to your friend. Then to Desmond. Then to you."

Lij's arm slackened like a flower left too long in the heat.

When the boulevard cleared, Cayt dashed across, with

Lij trailing in hopping steps. She only had to make it to the edge of town. Her employer's contingency measurements would take care of the rest. She'd been eager to take on the assignment. All of the best operations went to more "seasoned agents," who just happened to be all men. She knew she had to take a chance to be noticed. So, when she proposed a covert op into the First Nations, it intrigued her director. The way she presented it, it was a no-lose situation: if she succeeded, they'd have the boy and a layout of Wewoka, an important border city. If she failed, they could disavow all knowledge of a rogue operative. And they'd be minus one meddlesome complainer.

They neared the edge of the city. The ruins of the ancient wall were in sight. Cayt fired three pulses into the air, waited, and fired three more. Instead of heading directly to the woods, she doubled back to follow a more circuitous pathway.

They soon reached a stand of trees. Ducking behind them, Cayt peered over a fallen trunk. She watched for the security patrols. A pack of steam-powered mechanical wolves went in the direction she almost headed in. Glancing toward the sky, she knew the mechanical hawks soared about but were less useful at night, especially through the canopy of the woods. Lij started to thrash about, so she wrapped her arms around him.

"It won't be much longer. I should have reinforcements arriving soon. They'll create enough ruckus for us to slip away."

In the cool of the night, Lij shivered in her arms.

"I know I'm supposed to do something," she said, watching him shake. Cayt slipped off her rifle coat and wrapped him with it. "I don't have any children of my own. Don't plan on having any. Which ain't to say I don't have fun trying."

Lij pulled the coat tighter around him.

"See? That was probably inappropriate. I just ain't the mothering type."

The sounds of men running about drew her attention. She cupped Lij's mouth and trained her weapon in the direction of their charge. They took up positions along the wall, on high alert. Exactly what she expected.

"You're scared, I bet. Don't be." Cayt stopped herself from saying that he'd be safe with her. No point in lying to the boy. She released his hand, tentative at first, nodding to Lij to see if he was going to cooperate and remain silent. He didn't quite nod. She still weighed whether she wanted to deliver him to her employer for the chance to prove herself to a bunch of men who thought nothing of her, or return the boy to the folks from Jamaica for the reward.

"Lord Melbourne is rather like your Mr. Coke, though I doubt either would see it. He found me when I was fourteen. Living in a shanty in some shithole part of a city God long forgot. Hiding in piles of garbage and debris, with my hidden stores of food cobbled together from restaurant leavings. I used to sneak into hotels and nick the food left on plates from people who ordered room service. Lord Melbourne caught me and brought me into his room. I thought he was going to beat me or . . . do things men with power do to people without it." Cayt's voice drifted off, caught between memories and regrets. "But he sat me down. Said that he saw something in me. A potential. He admired my resourcefulness and resilience. He convinced me to become a detective. That's what set me on the course to become a Pinkerton. I've been his ever since. Almost like a daughter."

Cayt stopped, wondering why she shared so much. Cover stories were tricky to keep straight, which was why it helped to create ones laced with the truth. She never felt comfortable opening up about herself, yet she found herself exposed before Lij. Him and his funny green eyes.

"From what I hear, you and me are a lot alike. Both had folks muck around with our innards. Making us into something . . . more. A phrenologist. Heh. I was young and dumb. They fiddled around with my mind."

Cayt flipped her head forward and removed her blond wig. Her head was smooth underneath. A scar creased the side of her skull just above her ear. Lij ran his finger along the scar. Cayt startled at first, almost pulled away. But she relaxed and let the boy trace the length of her wound.

"I can whisper to folks just like we were talking, except without moving our lips," she said with her mind before switching back to using her lips. "And if I concentrate real hard, I can 'push' someone. That's what I call it. Sort of like suggesting something, like when I had my guard undo my handcuffs. Can't do that very often, though. I'm all nosebleeds and headaches afterwards. Yeah, powerful folks mess with us like we don't matter none. They can't just let us be. We become weapons in their war. Not that I can talk. I don't do all the politics well. During our last disagreement, I shot my last superintendent in the leg."

Lij followed her eyes. His body less tense.

"You seem to settle down when I'm talking. You must like stories."

Lij nodded.

"Well, I'm not much of a storyteller, but it's going to take some time for my people to come collect us, and I'm not going to truss you up to keep you from fussing. My grandmother was from the old country. Now, they could spin a good fairy tale. Don't ask me why, but this one here was one of my favorites . . .

There once was a man with only the clothes on his back to

his name. He was a good feller, an honest man, and lived life by his simple duty. Then one day, a young 'un comes into his life. The man worked mighty hard night and day to provide them bread but knew it wasn't enough. He decided to find a godparent for this child.

The man wandered along the great highway and paused at a crossroads. Now he says to himself that the first person he meets, he would ask to be the child's godparent. Not too long after, a man approached him.

"Poor man, I know your heart and what troubles you. Your yoke is heavy. Cast it to me. Not only will I relieve your burden, but I will raise this one here as if he were my own. He will know peace on earth," the stranger said.

"Who are you?" the man asked.

"I am God."

"Then I don't want to have you as the godparent. I don't understand your high-faluting wisdom. I have seen the good starve in the streets and the bad prosper. I have seen only the injustice which you allow."

And so the man turned his back on the Almighty.

The man continued his trek along the great highway. His journey took him all across strange lands. Again, he paused at a crossroads and waited on the first person he would meet. A man soon approached him.

"I know what you seek. You desire freedom for you and your child. Freedom to do what you want. I can grant you

that, and in so doing, I can give him great wealth and all the joys this world has to offer."

"Who are you?" the man asked.

"I am the Devil."

"Then I don't want to have you as the godparent, either. I don't pretend to understand your lies. But I do know this: I have seen the selfishness of people and the cruelty they offer as they seek their own ends. Sometimes, folks just don't know any better and you lead them astray by their own desires."

And so the man turned his back on Ol' Scratch.

The man took up his journey along the great highway, determined to find a suitable godparent for the boy he called his own. When he had traveled a great distance, he came to another crossroads. He waited. A woman approached him. A fair though quite ordinary lady.

"Take me as his godmother." The woman had no pretense about her.

"Who are you?"

"I am Death. I make all equal."

"Now, you take the poor as well as the rich. The young as well as the old, don't matter what their station or standing. You are the right one."

"Then I shall make the boy famous. His gifts can be used to heal the world."

When the boy grew older, Death brought the young man to her home. She conducted him into the underworld, down into a series of great vaults. Inside were candles of all sorts of lengths. Only the unlit candles were very large. She reached for a small candle which had nearly burnt out.

"Look here. I have the duration of everyone's life. I hold them dear to me, but when that final flame fades"—she snuffed the flame between her thumb and forefinger—"I claim them."

"Is my candle here?" the young man asked.

"Everyone's candle is here. But I have brought you here to show you your gift. I'll make you a celebrated physician. When you are with a patient, I shall always appear to you. Now, if I stand by the head of the patient, you can tell them that, without a doubt, they are going to be healed. If I stand by their feet, then there is nothing they can say, do, or pray, I shall claim them. Do you understand?"

"Yes," he said, though his eyes never left the dancing flames of the candles.

Soon, he became the most famous physician in the world. It was rumored that all he had to do was glance in a patient's direction and know how they were going to turn out. Far and wide, people came to this here famous doctor.

One day, a great baron became ill. He was a shrewd businessman with money and power and contacts. It was said that all knowledge found its way to the baron's fingertips. He knew the secrets men vowed to take with them to the grave. So great was his influence that even kings feared his outstretched hand. He summoned the young man. When the young man came into the bedchamber, the baron held up his hand.

"How close is Death?" the old man asked.

The young man couldn't help but glance at Death as she stood at the baron's feet.

The old man held up his hand again, silencing the young man before he could pronounce his condition. The baron snapped his fingers and his attendants rushed to him. He whispered his orders to them and they wheeled his bed around so that now Death stood at his head.

"Now tell me my fate," the baron said, his mouth a-grinning like a wolf ready to pounce.

The young man pronounced that the baron should live. He anointed the old man with ointments, and soon the baron's health returned.

Now you see, the way Death saw it, the baron had bound her and used her for his own purposes, so she grew dark with anger and she had to take it out on someone.

"All is over for you," she said to the young man. "A candle was meant to grow dark this day, and if not his, then the lot falls to you."

Death had to be true to herself and to her calling, no matter how unfair it might seem to the young man. With that, they returned to the cave beneath the earth. Thousands upon thousands of candles flickered in the dark.

"Show me the flame of my life," the young man said.

Death picked up a small one whose flame threatened to go out with the merest movement. "Here."

"Blessed godmother, if you ever loved me or cared for me even a li'l bit, light me a new candle."

"I cannot. The baron had made a new candle for himself with yours. One must go out as another is lit." She raised her thumb and forefinger to the flame. There Death wavered.

"How do you think the story should end?" Cayt asked. "Does Death simply snuff out the young man's candle, his life having run its course? That's fair, right? Maybe it was just his time to put himself in her lap for a final sleep? Should Death take hold of a new candle and light it with the old? Maybe the young man escapes Death to find someone new to instruct him in the ways of his gift? Does another sacrifice himself for the young man? You see, that's the thing about old stories: the endings get retold so many times, depending on the audience, that it's difficult to remember how it should go."

Lij turned away from her and rocked back and forth. The strange boy fascinated her. This was the one who brought countries to the brink of cold war with one another. The businesses and their executive officers bent decree and oath to secure for their own interests. Though he was no more than a package for her to deliver, Cayt had to admit to a certain amount of curiosity about him.

And she had a way of peeking inside of this particular package without leaving any trace.

"I don't know if you're worth all the nuisance." She knelt down on one knee in front of him. "Let me see what all the fuss is about."

She stared into Lij's eyes. Taking a deep breath, she closed her eyes and opened her thoughts to seek out his mind. Crossing the blackness between them, she swam through the ether, that connecting space between people. As she headed toward him, she met a wall of resistance. She hadn't encountered anything like it since she had last trained with other adepts. On the horizon of her mind, a dark cloud beckoned her in. The yawning abyss threatened to devour her. The earth ripped out from under her; her mind tumbled through the ether. The space thickened, like fingers wrapping into a fist around her as her mind collapsed onto his. His green eyes filled her. Bits of her personality broke off into shards, her memories fragmenting such that she couldn't tell hers from the boy's. Unmade in an instant, then stitched back together. Reduced to an idea. Potential. Possibility. Oblivion.

VII.

Tomorrow People

THE WIND RUSTLED THROUGH the leaves. Thunder rumbled from the woods, deep and hideous. Desmond, Inteus, and Kajika stood before the great wooden doors. Wewoka glittered before them under the chilly night sky. Security officers rushed about in search of Cayt.

"Do you hear it?" Inteus asked.

"A storm comes," Kajika said.

"A storm of war." Inteus turned to her. "You must remain here."

They didn't bother switching to their native language. Desmond didn't know whether he should step away to allow them a moment of privacy.

"This better not be any of your masculine preening," she said.

"It's my practical nature. You are a leader as well as with child."

"Your child."

"And as your chief of security, my duty to our child,

you, and our village is to keep you all safe."

"Come back safe or . . ."

" . . . I know. 'Shits Like Deer.'" Inteus kissed her.

Kajika laid her hand to his heart, then pushed him away. Inteus signaled two guards to follow her. Warriors continued to take up positions, armed and ready.

"You'll need these." Inteus snapped his fingers twice. One of his men brought out Desmond's cane and the Colt Mustang.

"Now I'm dressed for the occasion," Desmond said.

Inteus and Desmond rushed to the courtyard. They stopped short when they saw what stormed the city.

A tide of steammen washed up on Wewoka. Military prototypes, more sophisticated than the automata of Tejas, but there was something dangerous about them. Like madmen woken from night terrors, something about the steammen was wrong. The lead troops had faces like a series of blank plates. Their builders barely bothered to make them look human. Rather, they appeared more like helmeted soldiers. Large eyes, like recessed headlamps, visible from the shadow of their visors. Brass casing tubes ran from their necks to their chassis like bulging veins. A thin trail of smoke issued from their packs. Like miniature cities, they were all mechanical force and clouds of noxious fumes. A series of valves and knobs calibrating their steam engines prevented stealthy movement. But stealth wasn't the point. Their noise, like Albion's red jackets of yore, announced their presence in order to terrorize their enemy. Gleaming in the moonlight like knights to the rescue, their march an iron synchronicity. The strange song of machine noise clanged like a hymn of pistons and gears. They brought their weapons to bear at the same time and fired balls of revolving fire, miniature stars careening into space.

The next wave brought heavier units like walking tanks. One of their arms fixed with a pulse cannon, the other little more than a mechanical pincer. Hydraulics hissed with each stuttering step. The Union Jack emblazoned their chests like a red, white, and blue target. Their top swiveled, disengaged at the waist to spin about to lock onto a target.

Last was their colossus steamman. Like a personalized locomotive, a mountain of machinery billowed smoke. Human troops attended its zombie-like ambling, running up and down the ladders along its spine. It spilled coal dust as it moved, like an ancient traveler brushing the dirt from their cloak during the course of their travels. Fitted with a dozen arms, each tipped with blades like metal scorpion tails.

The procession of steammen clanked along the sidewalks. They moved at a slow, steady pace, unhurried by the pulse fire showered on them by Inteus's troops. A few human operatives ran among the robotic drones, flanking them as they thundered down the boulevard. Some men had modifications similar to Inteus's, though the gears and chains that powered the muscles of their limbs had been left exposed. Again, the attachments were cruder than those of Inteus's, perhaps in the early stages of development. Their mechanical limbs attached to a brace, which fastened at the collar and ran to the waist.

If part of him was aware that he was in the sights of an assassin's weapon, Desmond was long past listening to it. Inteus slammed into him, knocking him out of the path of fire. The wave of heat from the near miss focused Desmond's attention. Inteus fired once, then twice. The marksman's body tumbled off the nearby roof. Giving a slight hitch to his shoulder, Inteus dislocated his arm and spun it around like a mace of death. Generous arcs slammed into soft bodies and cracked skulls.

From the cover of trees, Seminoles stepped into the clearing and fired. Groups of men provided cover fire while others gathered any bystanders out of harm's way. Up close, the Seminoles were little to no match for the steammen, but their weapons outranged the steammen's more powerful weapons. Trained to fight in units, a group of Seminoles scrambled together. They shot handheld pulse cannons, only firing a handful of shots before dispersing and then regrouping at another location.

The steammen marched toward the nearest mushroom-shaped water reclamation unit. A group of operatives deployed toward the structure. The men ignored the steammen as they fired at the shadows where the Seminoles were. One man began to photograph the structure. The others quickly set to dismantle its faceplating to get a better look inside.

Industrialists.

Desmond flew into a rage. The steammen were glorified distraction, cover for Cayt and espionage agents to gather intelligence. Two soldiers emerged into the light. Desmond leapt onto them. He broke the first one's neck before grabbing the rifle of the second when the man struggled to bring it to bear. Desmond flung the weapon aside. He headbutted the man. The man's fingers slipped loose of the rifle. Desmond turned it around and fired at the man. Other soldiers came. Desmond fired at them. The rifle's recoil kicked like a nanny goat, nearly wrenching Desmond's shoulder. He wasn't sure where his shots landed. Somewhere along the treeline, shadows bobbed and weaved. The next shots cut down one man and scattered the rest. Desmond made his way back to Inteus's side.

"We need to end this now," Inteus said.

"Agreed. Reinforcements might be coming."

"I'll take the fight out of them."

Desmond nodded. "I need to find Lij."

"Though we are of different tribes, tonight you are as my own brother."

Desmond clasped his hand. "Watch your step and walk good."

Desmond provided cover for Inteus and his men.

Inteus launched two campaigns. The first offensive charged the initial wave of steammen and their attending soldiers. Flanked by mechanical wolves, a column of warriors swarmed against the force of steammen. The second outmaneuvered the relief column, cutting the steammen from one another. A series of ambushes and quick raids, not giving the enemy a fixed point to focus on.

"Yohoehoo!" Inteus's war cry began as a growl but ended as a shrill yelp. He charged the colossus, almost too fast to keep sight of. A whir of blades and metal ground against one another. Its nearest arm swung but was blocked by Inteus's left arm. He tried to spin in order to position himself for a close-range shot but was equally hampered. Inteus slashed while the robot pivoted and whirred its arms. Neither found an advantage in such close quarters.

The metal beast churned in fury, its arms pistoning in attack, like fan blades spinning in desperate arcs. Inteus bobbed between metal arms, not retreating an inch but overmatched by the gleaming monstrosity. Their moves attuned to one another, the picture of slow grace. Inteus' movements were as fluid as the forms of *bangaran*; it was a mesmerizing display.

Steam rose from the boiler sheltered in the beast's chest. The overworked chassis nearly glowed red from the heat. Avoiding one of the whipping blades, Inteus fell against it. He screamed as blisters creased his back.

Inteus jammed his left arm into the underbelly of the automata and fired. The pumps wheezed and slowed, the gears shuddered to a halt. Its stacks mewled, the sound of steam escaping the punctured tank. Its body slowed, then slumped. Iron fingers grasped at the night air until all movement stopped.

Bursting through the smoke and flames, Desmond stalked the streets. Explosions kicked up dirt all around him. He gave the hilt of his cane a twist and freed his blade and dropped his scabbard. His sword in one hand, the Colt Mustang in the other, he cursed as a few men rushed him, but he separated them from their limbs with quick dispatch. No doubt they would turn up on a future battlefield with mechanical limbs and a hatred for all things flesh.

Desmond scanned the area for any hint of Cayt and Lij. His instinct was to head directly to the woods. After a few jogged steps in that direction, he stopped. Something wasn't right. The movement of the steammen, their angle of approach . . . someone waiting on their arrival wouldn't hide directly in the path of two clashing forces. He headed toward the rear of the ruined wall line.

Desmond entered the woods, then slowed. The woods looked so different at night. He knew they were near, could almost feel them. Somewhere in the dark, Cayt stalked him, preparing for her attack. Desmond quieted his mind for battle and measured her movements. Young and fast, she would be a serpent in combat. He pictured her with a blade flicked out to slash his throat, her movements mercurial and spidery. A feint to lure him within striking distance. Him barely avoiding her kicks. Her retreating to the edge of his vision, attacking from his blind spots. Him dancing out of the way of her blows. He'd have to be wary of her hands, quick to draw her guns in less than a breath. Maybe she'd raid his mind to distract him.

"You're old and weak. Couldn't even keep the boy safe."

Desmond stepped to the edge of a clearing. "I'm here. Where are you?"

"Around," Cayt said from the shadows. Her voice was off. Almost afraid.

"Not going to show yourself?" Desmond held up the Colt Mustang. "I have something of yours."

"The boy is across from you. Take him and go." Her voice trailed from the shadows.

"I don't understand."

"The boy is dangerous."

"Only as dangerous as an idea," Desmond said.

"Some ideas should remain . . . ideas." Cayt sounded tired now. "I thought about killing him."

"But you didn't."

"Just as I could have killed you as you approached."

Desmond set the Colt Mustang on the ground and backed toward the boy. "Some ideas, even dangerous ones, need a chance to develop."

Without so much as a snapped twig, he knew she was gone. So was her Colt Mustang.

A figure shivered against a fallen tree. Wrapped in the woman's jacket, Lij rocked back and forth. He cupped his hands over his ears and kept his eyes shut. Desmond kept his back to the boy, still half-expecting an ambush, but one never came.

"Lij, it's me. Desmond. Only me."

The boy continued to rock. The sounds of the firefight began to subside.

"It's okay, Lij." Desmond hugged the boy. "It'll all be okay."

VIII.

Many Rivers to Cross

IN THE EARLY MORNING, Desmond found a spot he liked—within sight of his *chickee* but surrounded by trees and a creek. If the sun hit him at the right angle and he closed his eyes, it reminded him of Jamaica. A brown bird with an orange breast approached. It eyed him rue-fully. As if not considering him a threat, it began to scrape at the dirt. It pecked a small, dirt-encrusted worm and gripped it like a lost treasure. It cast one last glance at Desmond, checking to see if he were after its prize. Hop-ping off, not bothering to take flight, it opted to dine out of sight.

Lost in his own thoughts, Desmond no longer felt hunted. He had a chance to tour one of the mines and thought about working there. Work might make him feel useful again, make him feel connected. If only to be able to approach people again without them having that hint of fear in their eyes.

He left the Seminoles alone to bury their dead. The

death ritual struck him as important, a very private affair not welcoming to strangers. The entire family of each warrior mourned for four days. On the fourth morning, they used the herbs the medicine man made to either drink with tea or wash with. Their widows wore black and mourned for four moons. Once the body was placed, family would abandon the camp and leave the deceased to make their journey. They took the belongings of their loved one who had passed away and threw each item into the river. To hold onto a loved one's possessions was to hinder their journey and hold them back.

Desmond knew a portion of what they felt. To have the carpet suddenly pulled out from under him and become lost in emptiness. That sense of drowning that came with simply trying to make it through another day. In the past months, he had tried to find meaning in having his home ripped from him. If only to fill the void in his heart, to complete those inner spaces so that he could at least breathe again. That was the thing about shared loss. Total strangers could open themselves up. They could share wisdom. They could muddle through the dark times together and cling to hope.

"Someone was looking for you." Kajika strolled along the path, holding Lij's hand. His free arm clutched a new cornhusk doll.

"I thought I'd be back before you woke," Desmond

said to Lij. "I'm sure Kajika had more important things to do than walk a lost pickney."

"It's all right. I needed a break." Kajika let go of Lij's hand. The boy skittered off to play in the grass. "Preparations are well underway for the Green Corn Dance. They don't need me for that."

"Is that the 'busk' everyone was talking about?"

"Yes. It's the centerpiece of our purification ceremonies. It symbolizes renewal and forgiveness. Think of is as a series of commitment rituals. You might like the stomp dances. It's also customary to select young men as future leaders or shaman."

"Inteus healing well?"

"Too slowly, by his measure. Our doctors wanted to keep him a little longer, but he'd hear none of it. He's already overseeing repairs and doubling our security measures."

"The incursion was an attempted coup d'état effectively, correct? It constitutes an act of war?"

"Albion declare war on one of the mightiest nations on the planet? Not even at the height of their madness. What was it Regent James Madison once said? 'It is prudent such attempts should be concealed as well as suppressed.'"

"Surely, someone has to be called into account," Desmond said.

"I assure you, no evidence will be traced back to Cayt's employer. Or any high-ranking Albion official."

"And who knows where Cayt disappeared to."

"Inteus's men tracked her as best they could, but she seems to have dropped out of sight."

"So, besides her vanishing within your borders, which no one could admit to—"

"Admit? Because the letter of the law would stop them from reprisals? It's their version of attempting to play by the rules they themselves set out for 'civilized nations.' You see how well they adhere to their laws." Kajika turned to Lij. "But there are plenty of days ahead for talk of politics. I thought I'd return this wayward one to you."

"Thank you," Desmond said in the Creek language.

"You're getting better." Kajika turned and headed back.

Lij sat in the grass and played with his doll. Desmond crouched down beside him.

"How do you feel about being here?" Desmond asked.

"I don't know."

"Are you enjoying being around people a little more?"

"Fifty-three percent."

"Where would you rather be?"

Lij mumbled a series of noises. He reminded Desmond of a mechanical calculator working through a problem but getting stuck.

"Are you scared?" Desmond asked.

The boy shook his head.

"I know what that feels like. It feels like we've been running all of our lives. I think you've been on the run longer than you've known any home. I'm sorry for that. But there are people after you. They don't see themselves as bad. They may even think they have good reasons, but they are just selfish. You deserve the right to live your life and make your own choices. You're so different in how you come at the world. I just want to protect that."

A deer stopped short of where they talked. Unsure where to step, it didn't near, but it didn't flee either as Desmond stared at it. Finally, it took wary laps at the gentle-running stream. Perhaps catching their scent, it turned Desmond's way. Studied him with passing fascination.

"This might be as good a place to call home as any. 'As a dog wags its tail, its heart well.' What do you think?"

Lij stopped playing, a thoughtful pause while he was locked in his internal deliberation.

"Home." Lij pointed to Desmond. "*You* are my home. You keep my stories safe."

Acknowledgments

This entire journey began with my mother telling me about a place in Jamaica that only allowed "outsiders" in one time a year. A "tale of two Jamaicas," as it were. So, this book wouldn't be possible without my mother (who still probably won't read this, but she'll love that I thanked her, so that should give me a pass for at least one Mother's Day gift).

I'd also like to thank my wife and sons, who continue to support me and my need to tell stories. Thank you for your continued love, faith, and support. They also had to endure a research trip to Jamaica. Be strong, fam!

I'd also love to thank my writers group at the Harrison Art Center. You all were wonderfully savage on the early drafts of this and this wouldn't be here without you.

Publishing with Tor has been a dream of mine. Their staff and artists (THAT COVER ART! Shout-out to Jon Foster and Christine Foltzer) are a great team of professionals. But I'd especially like to thank the great Lee Harris. It's always a pleasure to work with him, and

I always take comfort when I know my words are in his hands.

Lastly, a special "thank you" to my amazing agent, Jen Udden. You make this publishing journey a whole lot less scary.

About the Author

Photograph by Larissa Johnson

With more than fifty stories, **MAURICE BROADDUS**'s work has appeared in *Lightspeed Magazine, Weird Tales, Apex Magazine, Asimov's, Cemetery Dance, Black Static,* and many more. He is the author of the urban fantasy trilogy the Knights of Breton Court. He coauthored the play *Finding Home: Indiana at 200.* His novellas include *I Can Transform You, Orgy of Souls, Bleed with Me,* and *Devil's Marionette.* He is the coeditor of *Dark Faith, Dark Faith: Invocations, Streets of Shadows,* and *People of Colo(u)r Destroy Horror.* He lives in Indianapolis, Indiana, surrounded by family, friends, and a cat named Ferb. Learn more about him at MauriceBroaddus.com.

TOR·COM

Science fiction. Fantasy. The universe.

And related subjects.

*

More than just a publisher's website, *Tor.com* is a venue for **original fiction, comics,** and **discussion** of the entire field of SF and fantasy, in all media and from all sources. Visit our site today—and join the conversation yourself.

CPSIA information can be obtained
at www.ICGtesting.com
Printed in the USA
FSOW02n2225050517
33920FS